The Thinning

Minister Gretchen Harris

outskirtspress
DENVER, COLORADO

I dedicate this work of love

to

My Lord and Savior Jesus Christ

My parents

(Deceased)

Wilbur R. Dooley

&

Blanche Williamson Dooley

My husband and partner of 30 years

Minister Robert K. Harris

(Twin Sisters) Elder Anita Dooley

&

Missionary Annette Harris

(Children) Demario, Eric, Robert, Danielle a.k.a. Alex and Corey

(a Host of Grandkids)

To

The entire Harris, Rodriguez-Negron & Smith clan

My Pastors Jeff and Deborah Carter (Ephesus Ministries)

Minister Linda Combs

Sis Jackie, and all of my dear friends and loved ones for your support

(Last and not least)

The precious Holy Ghost, who took my hand in His,

And He spoke into my spirit, these words of hope for the hopeless

'Thinning Prose'

Twins of the spirit
A mold created and broken
By the same mighty hands
Darkness and light
Dimness and bright
Who can know the mind of The Lord?
Who can discern His purpose?
Good and evil
He created one as well as the other
A soulful Battle
One lives as well as the other
Two shall die for the of good of the one
To break loose the grip of the riches of this life
Has not God Himself allowed this thing?
Twins of the soul
A Thinning has happened
And still I ask
Has not God Himself allowed this marvelous
thing?

(Foreword)

I am continually amazed by the way that God teaches the world about His definition of love. The church is long overdue for a demonstration of what God meant when He said "To love one another". Conditioned for years by denominational doctrine and the complacency of quoting a scripture or two, the church falls short when faced with the challenge of displaying this most important attribute of Jesus Christ. But what happens when the real love of God calls for more than giving a familiar scripture or a hug or the typical, "I'll be praying for you?" How much are we willing to sacrifice for the love of a soul?

As the return of the Lord Jesus Christ draws near, we are faced with a world in which the magnitude of evil is unfathomable. Why would God command us to love a child molester, a rapist, or a serial killer? Even those who are "spiritually minded" find it challenging to love in deed and truth. And yet, God continues to compel and command us to love. "And this commandment we have from Him, that he who loveth God, love his brother also." 1 John 4:21. As I read "The Thinning", I was never before so aware of how much I needed to confront my own heart about the lack of love it has for humanity. I cried as I realized how I had learned to justify not loving those deemed unlovable by the world's standard. I cried as I realized that my own soul needed a "Thinning."

On my face in the presence of God, I finally realized that the only love that can save this world from eternal damnation is the love of another human being, more than the love of self. It must be a love that can see beyond the evil wickedness of an individual's deeds and that can reach for the tortured soul trapped inside. God is calling for the only love that can save this world today. He is calling for Agape love. A songwriter once asked the question, "What's love got to do with it?" The answer is, everything, and more than our finite minds could ever truly comprehend.

Minister Gretchen Harris presents to us, "The Thinning." "For God so loved the world, that He gave His only begotten Son..." John 3:16. What are you willing to give?

Elder Anita Dooley

(Prologue)

Thirty seconds shy of midnight on October 31, 1977 in two separate hospital rooms at the St. Augustus Community Hospital in Augusta Georgia, two women, who were complete strangers, were in the final pangs of childbirth. One woman was Hispanic and the other was Caucasian. Both women were mere minutes away from delivering male babies. Both had married at a young age. Both were close to age thirty. This is where their similarities ended. The Hispanic woman was in the process of bearing child number six, while the Caucasian woman and her Jamaican born husband had finally conceived after ten years of heartbreak. This was because of a rare genetic blood disorder in the wife's family tree. They were shocked and thrilled to be new parents. They had so many plans for this miracle baby. Thirty seconds before midnight both babies tumbled into the waiting hands of their residents and were passed to a nearby nurse. Neither baby cried or struggled as they were wiped, examined, swaddled and handed to their excited parents. Both boys had excellent vital signs and were whole and very handsome sons. The Hispanic child was olive toned with a well shaped head covered with thick, silky, dark locks. His dark smoke colored eyes were well shaped and evenly spaced. The part Caucasian, and Jamaican child had an equally well shaped head with a forest of curly red hair and translucent blue eyes, which glowed with a keen intelligence beyond his age. Later, when comparing accounts, the witnesses of both births agreed that it was very odd and unsettling that each of the babies never uttered one sound as they searched the curious faces peering at them. They each appeared to be trying to locate something...or someone.

Hundreds of miles away in a college dormitory a young seminary student of Irish descent, fretted over a very serious term paper. The very thick term paper dealt with an ancient sect of monks and a secret practice that included a crystallite. At thirty seconds to midnight he felt an overwhelming unction in his spirit to gather all of his painstakingly collected data and earnestly pray over it. As was his nature concerning his faith... he immediately obeyed.

Over a thousand miles away, a young Indian psychology student tossed and turned with troubled sleep. She was agonizing over which topic to choose for her first human case study. At precisely thirty seconds before midnight she popped awake so suddenly that she careened out of her small fold away cot and banged her head on her cherished Hindu statue. Snapping her fingers she spoke to her indifferent companion, "I've got it. My topic will be, *The Making of a Sociopath.*" If she had, had any inkling of the places that her choice of study was going to take her... she would have run for her life.

In that very same maternity ward at St. Augustus Hospital, fifteen minutes after midnight, a beautiful, chocolate brown baby girl with thick, dark, curly hair, hazel, almond shaped eyes and deep dimples, was in the beginning stages of letting her newly introduced parents know that she did not appreciate being removed from the comfort of her previous dwellings. No matter how much they kissed her, cooed at her or rocked her, she stated her objections. She would continue to state her case...for months and months to come.

And the children sang, as they chased each other through the dense rubber trees, "The Rag tree man's gonna get you, the Rag tree man's gonna get you. He'll cut your neck and drink your blood, the Rag tree man's gonna get you!"

"Forty years later...."

"Oh Riya, the Rag tree man was real all the time. He was real!"

Chapter 1
'The Day I Met Ricky Plain'

"Two pounds of washing powder two pounds of soap, who's not ready holler, billygoat." Twelve year old, Katydids, (Katrina) Jewel Brewster froze in her hide n go seek call, to openly stare at the family moving into the two story house at the end of her block. Her twelve year old senses took in the worn furniture making its way on the backs of strange looking, strange speaking people. They were what caused her to forget her rigorously taught manners. Their skin was olive colored (her mom used that word to describe the Hispanic family to her later). They had a variety of straight and curly hair dos. Surprisingly though, even these unusual neighbors did not do to Katrina what the object her infatuation did to her heart strings. Suddenly, kicked to the curb were her thoughts of hide n go seek, hop scotch and tagging along with papa to the corner store. The object of her total fixation was a slightly built, curly headed Hispanic boy with a serious scowl on his face. Drawn towards him by irresistible cords, her feet took into the territory of her first case of puppy love. Katrina's playmates were completely forgotten as she zeroed in on her target. The unfamiliar words going in and out of the house took on a muted quality as she came face to face with the object of her adoration. Studying the boy's face with suddenly dry, cherry lollipop stained lips and blushing furiously, Katrina blurted out, "Hi, what's your na...?" The boy came close up to Katrina's startled face and with the most evil look she had ever seen, said, "I don't like you, you give me a pain, for your information I go by the name *RICKY PLAIN.*""ANZEL," yelled a large woman with a thick accent and her arms full of pillows. "Get your skinny little tail in the house now." "Vamoose!" The boy gave Katrina one more hateful look and ran into the house. The woman smiled apologetically at Katrina and disappeared behind the boy. She was too young to understand the pitter patter of it all...but Katydids was in love for life.

Anzel Martinez leaned over and traced the milk chocolate outline of his beloved wife Katrina's face. Still sleeping, she wriggled her nose and her full lips curled at the corners. Delighted, Anzel chuckled and dove at her covering her face with wet, sloppy kisses. "Hey, hey, stop handsome, what are you doing? Why you always messing with me when I'm trying to get my beauty sleep?" She said with feigned aggravation. Anzel put on his most serious face and countered with, "So you really don't remember what day it is eh muchacha?" Watching Katrina's beautiful hazel eyes become as round as saucers, Anzel lost his composure and burst out laughing. "Oh Anzel, oh baby, did I forget our wedding anniversary? Oh my sweet tamale." Abruptly she stopped talking when she realized that Anzel was laughing. He was laughing so hard that he was almost falling out of bed. Seriously not amused, Katrina narrowed her eyes and readied a snappish retort when Anzel threw up both hands in surrender and said, "before you fire those hot tacos, remember that you're the one who forgot the most important day of my life, Mrs. Martinez." He threw in for good measure. Anzel and Katrina were well on the way to building a very compatible marriage. Earlier they came up with a system to base everything about their marriage on the word of God. They gave communication with each other top priority. Whenever they had a serious issue to work through, their secret signal for absolute truth and focus was, "I go by the name of Ricky Plain." Smiling sheepishly, Katrina reached out a freshly manicured nail and traced Anzel's handsome face. "Okay, my big strong, hombre," she said coyly. "What is the funny, ha, ha?" Anzel eased out of the bed making sure to put some distance between them and said, "Today's not our anniversary, tomorrow is, my chili con carne." Knowing it was coming, he ducked as a pillow whizzed past his head. Following the pillow, Katrina launched herself at Anzel, barely landing in his arms. Her shrill laughter froze in her throat when she saw that Anzel was staring at the floor in open mouthed shock. Looking down in puzzlement she began to scream as her eyes followed a large pool of blood that shimmered on the floor as it was being fed from her pajama pant leg. "Anzel, help me." Before he could secure his hold on her…she slipped to the floor in a dead faint.

"C'mon, chili con carne, you have to eat something, you need your strength." Katrina turned to glare at Anzel, but he had such a comical look on his face; she dissolved into giggles. Unfortunately, the heaping teaspoon of congealing oatmeal just inches from her nose caused Katrina to violently dry heave. She jumped up and made a mad dash for the bathroom, slamming the door firmly behind her. Six weeks had passed since that frightening scare the day before their wedding anniversary. The couple had almost lost what they now knew to be an anticipated set of twins. Anzel secretly suspected that it was the power of suggestion that caused Katrina to develop morning sickness immediately upon finding out that she was pregnant. Yes his Katydids was a unique woman, and that was just the way he loved her. He doubted she would ever forget their wedding anniversary again, he knew he wouldn't. While listening to the sounds of her morning sickness routine, Anzel bowed his head and asked the Lord for the thousandth time to reveal the meaning of his tormenting nightmares. He'd been having the dreams sporadically since the day after he turned eighteen years old, but now they came frequently, with more intensity. He was worried about his mind, and didn't want to end up with early Alzheimer Disease like his dad had developed before he died a few years ago. The dream would always begin the exact same way. Always at night and Anzel would be walking down a garbage strewn street. He is always barefoot and in tattered clothing. The sound of his heart pounding in his chest fills his ears. So real. His shallow breathing makes fog characters in the air, as he passes the same group of people dressed in worse rags than his. Their repulsed expressions amaze him every time. Suddenly he is standing in front of a dilapidated building, and a rush of dread fills his heart. Sweat pops out on his forehead as he peers into the darkened interior. He whimpers as the blackness seems to reach through the broken windows to capture him. With a mind of their own his feet carry him up the cracked and leaning stairs and into the mouth of the monstrous building. Magically, as soon as he crosses the threshold, a pair of fancy, new shoes appear on his feet. Shiny wing tips, shoes he wouldn't choose to wear in a million years. Angry voices coming from the apartments to the left and right of him distract from his reluctant mission. Knowing what's coming next he struggles to keep his eyes averted from the door facing him at the end of the hallway. His eyes betray him and fix themselves on the door. Eerily, two numbers glow and pulsate, trying to convey some message. They are the numbers six and zero. He knows that the knob is slowly turning, in that dream knowledge way. His traitorous feet propel him towards the door as his heart threatens to explode in his chest from terror. Everything in Anzel fights to flee this place, but his relentless feet take him up to and through the now open apartment door. Anzel feels a pull in his spirit, something is drawing him. He hears a faint whisper, "Anzel, come and see, come in and see what real love looks like." Cautiously he enters a room which is completely bare except for a large, gilded mirror leaning against the wall and facing the door he'd just entered through. Once again Anzel's feet move him directly in front of the mirror. He glances anxiously over his shoulder knowing that now the door behind him will be solidly shut. "Nooo!" He cries out, trying to shut his eyes against what he knows is in the mirror. His eyes refuse to cooperate and he is soon peering into the image of every childhood nightmare and ghost story rolled up into one hideous ball. A snarling face, surrounded by filthy, wild red dreadlocks, or fur, stares back at Anzel. A pair of short, blunted horns, protrude from each side of its head. The teeth are ragged, decaying and dripping with blood, but it's the eyes that horrify Anzel the most, and haunt his waking hours. The maddened, hate filled eyes, lit with an eerie, pale blue light. They bore right into Anzel's tender soul. It's the sheer terror of what happens next that mercifully sends Anzel back to blessed reality. Anzel slowly reaches both of his hands up to touch his own face, and feels two horns protruding from his own head. The creature laughs and whispers, "Welcome....home...brother." Just remembering the dream causes Anzel to break out in chill bumps and shake uncontrollably. Katrina's voice brings him out of his deep revelry. "Anzel? Poppy, what's wrong? Is it the dreams again?" Through his tearstained, troubled eyes Anzel sees Katrina's concern and fear. "Baby, you have got to talk to somebody professional. You know, a Christian professional." Grabbing both of Katrina's hands, Anzel buries his face in them. Filled with an overwhelming sense of dread she can barely make out what Anzel is mumbling, but she wagers by the familiar rhythm that he is praying. Doing what comes naturally…they pray until the peace of God fills them and the entire house.

Scarcely aware of the bustling hospital atmosphere Anzel wrung his hands together to the amusement of pastor and friend Dijin Morgant Lockhart. Dijin feigned a yawn to keep from chuckling at his anxious friend's expense. The agitated Anzel was beginning sentences in Spanish and finishing them in English. Laughing out loud now Dijin said, "Please, brother sit down before you wear a hole in your shoes. Seriously Anzel, sit, sit." Catching the serious note in his pastor's voice, he reluctantly sat. Pastor Dijin cleared his throat a bit nervously and said, "Listen Anzel, I am going to bring up a subject with you that I know is going to make you uncomfortable." Anzel popped out of his seat saying, "Did the doctor say something about Katrina or the twins? Why won't they let me back in there?" Trying not to smile Dijin said, "You were feeling a little faint, remember? Katrina's fine. She's got at least two aunts as well as her mother to hold down the fort." Anzel blushed from the subtle way Dijin mentioned his near fainting spell. Marveling at the pink tinge to Anzel's cheeks, he continued, "Brother Martinez, don't worry, after our first child was born I told Ella that she would have to excuse me from anymore. I think she was more relieved than I was." Taking a sip of water he continued carefully, "Your wife mentioned to me that you've been having some powerful dreams." Quickly he added, "She didn't go into details, she only asked me to mention it to you." The stubborn look that came over Anzel's face caused Dijin to try a different approach. "That gorgeous young lady sure loves you a lot man. You are truly one blessed hombre." Anzel's countenance softened and his eyes twinkled as his love for Katrina filled his heart. Before he could reply to his pastor's obvious ploy, a scrub nurse stuck her head into the waiting room and announced, "There are a set of the most beautiful twin girls I have ever seen waiting to meet their dad." She barely had enough time to clear the doorway before Anzel barreled through. He was standing next to Katrina and his two little angels before he remembered that he'd forgotten to thank his pastor and tell him goodbye, and it was much later before he remembered…that he was angry with Katrina for spilling his secret.

Chapter 2

"Rasta, Child of Sorrows"

Nine and a half year old Rasta Jones hid in the woods behind the brick Tudor homes that lined his middle class neighborhood. He lived in one of the identical homes with his much despised stepmother and her two wicked sons. Hearing the shrill, angry voice calling his name made him burrow deeper into the thick foliage. Viciously, she began to curse Rasta in her thick Patois' accent. From previous experience Rasta knew it was going to be a long, cold night. Yes, he would be sleeping in the woods once again. Although Rasta couldn't see his step mom he knew she would be dragging the long, heavy leather strap along the road, and he knew she would be grinning. At first their neighbors timidly tried to intervene on Rasta's behalf, but *"crazy Nadeene,"* as the entire neighborhood called his stepmother, would retaliate so viciously with cursing and threats of casting spells, they soon began to close their curtains, turn up their televisions and ignore the screams of a small frightened boy. There was one punishment in particular that Nadeene Jones derived pleasure from. She would allow Rasta only one item of food for weeks at a time. Usually it was cold creamed style corn from the can. She and her two natural sons would dine like royalty on smoked hams and fried chicken, along with elaborate desserts. Nadeene was an excellent cook and the owner of a Caribbean style restaurant. Rasta was not ever allowed to use the stove or microwave to warm his corn. What his step mom didn't know was that Rasta secretly learned to love the sweet, gooey vegetable. He developed an unnatural craving for it that would stay with him for the rest of his life. Trying to warm his cold fingers, the cast off child reached under his dingy, threadbare shirt and ran his fingers lightly along the raised scars on his chest and stomach which closely matched the ones on his back. Rasta hadn't shed a tear in over two years. Teaching himself not to show his pain and humiliation, he would secretly enjoy his step mom's frustration, then he would smile and sometimes laugh as the leather ripped and tore his tender skin in her fury. Looking at the darkening sky overhead Rasta let down his carefully constructed guard to ask, "Why me?" Turning away he shivered slightly as goose flesh broke out on his thin arms. *"Rasta."* The voices in the woods called softly to him. The voices used to frighten Rasta, but soon he began to seek them out. They fed the fury and rage and lust for revenge in his young heart. Rasta became greedy for what they had to share with him. They spoke of the thrill of rebellion and the power gained through fear. They showed Rasta how to turn things around for his own advantage. Rasta was a very willing pupil. He honed his hatred of his family into a sharp instrument. He hated his real mother who'd left him at the age of five, by dying from some strange blood sickness, and his father who'd married this evil witch and died shortly afterwards in a motorcycle accident. So much hatred for a small boy to bear. The voices encouraged this hate and seduced him into directing it towards God, but Rasta could never turn the full brunt of his anger in God's direction. Something would not allow him to completely hate God, confusion would fill his mind and a intense dread would paralyze him. Even the threats and lies from the voices wouldn't make him force the issue. After his father died Rasta quickly learned how despised he was for his pale color, red hair and blue eyes. His new name became "dat devil boy." He was an startling contrast to the milk and dark chocolate hues of his step family. As the evil in Rasta's heart grew he paid his dues to the voices in the secret, bloody, satanic rites required for his evil education. Small neighborhood pets began to disappear. The neighborhood's response was to look the other way, keep their children close at hand and pray to a variety of deities. The demons shrieked with glee at the feeble attempts for protection. So after Rasta had gotten his basic training in the field of evil, and feeling like a man by the tender age of eleven, he decided it was time to strike back…hard.

The 911 call came in at approximately 9:00 p.m. The overworked dispatcher looked at the repeat address and sighed heavily. She quickly passed the hysterical information along and swallowed the sour taste in her mouth. Here was more trouble from that young Rasta Jones again. Rasta's violent episodes brought the police to their home on a regular basis. This time the police were confronted by a hysterical, bleeding woman and two disheveled teenage boys, along with a filthy, grinning Rasta. The woman spat blood and a loose tooth through swollen lips and said with her thick accent, "Ya gots ta tak dis devil boy outta my ouse!" Rasta felt a surge of power as he leapt at the frightened woman. Cursing her, he contemptuously tossed tufts of her hair on the ground. "Ah don carr wat ya do wit im, he can't cum bak ere." Staring at her with kind, weary eyes the older officer said, "Mam, you'll have to take that up with the juvenile court system because the boy is a mi……"

The distraught woman had already slammed the door shut in the police officer's faces, and they heard a definite lock click into place. Rasta spat on the welcome mat, and calmly walked out to the squad car and waited to be put in the back seat. The two officers looked at each other and shrugged. Rasta stared straight ahead and did not speak one word through the ride to headquarters, booking and finally lockdown. Seventy two hours later as Rasta was being booked into, the Linwood Facility for Boys, he decided to have his say. The twenty five year veteran, correction officer, slash receptionist, slash pastor, who thought that he had seen and heard it all; blushed three shades darker under Rasta's reawakening. He ran a finger over his pocket sized bible and muttered…"Have mercy Lord.

The Linwood Facility for Boys had been housing troubled boys for over fifty years. It was commonly used as a stepping stone to larger and more permanent institutions. The facility was home to an assortment of pathological liars, sociopaths, serial thieves, gang bangers and repeat rapist and murderers too young for the big house. Never before had Linwood experienced a complex mind like the child, Rasta Jones. Doctor Pila Thomas, resident psychiatrist, would literally shudder whenever Rasta entered her office for his weekly sessions. "C'mon Pila, he's just a child" , she would chastise herself sternly. She would swear on a stack of bibles, although she didn't believe in God. She would swear that there was no human emotion behind the cold stare of Rasta's pale blue eyes. When the strange youth smiled, which was rare, it never reached those unnerving eyes. Rasta's lips would curl into an almost feral smirk and he would sit very still and just look into your eyes. It had a most unsettling hypnotic effect. The older inmates had tried

to terrorize and beat Rasta into submission, but after countless attacks on Rasta, even to the point of badly fracturing his
arm, they began to avoid his hideously grinning face. Not very
long after they stopped, Rasta began his campaign of retaliation. It was swift and it was brutal. His calculated viciousness
defied all of Pila's medical knowledge. Pila had to sort through
all of the secret confessions of terrified inmates as she stayed
up many late nights searching for answers in her psychology
books. Not one of then held the answer to Rasta Jones. It was
amazing. These hardened, adult, children, born into drug in-
fested, abusive homes, tossed out to fend for themselves on
the cold heartless streets. Being unprotected by adults, they
were quickly recruited into prostitution and gang life to begin a career of drugs, murder and extortion. Never knowing
how to give or receive love, only knowing how to survive.
Astonishingly, these particular vendors of brutality came to
fear and dread the wrath of a one hundred pound, eleven year
old boy. Incredible, but seeing was believing. There was a new
wind blowing through Linwood Facility for Boys, and it was
foul and bent towards fatal...and it was just the way that Rasta
Jones liked it.

Doctor Pila Thomas wanted to scream. It was so darn de-
pressing to look at the thick files on the floor of her unkempt
office. The files contained ten years on Rasta Jones' reign of
terror in Linwood. He had literally used the facility for his
personal stomping ground. There were so many unresolved
incidents, so much anguish. The thing which bothered Pila the
most was the stubborn actions of the director of Linwood,
Doctor Jorge Maynard. He was responsible for approv-
ing the intense regimen, which Pila deemed necessary for

Rasta's rehabilitation. Instead he used his authority for under the counter payoffs to the parents and families of the emotionally and physically scarred inmates left behind in Rasta's wake. For him it was all about the reputation of the facility. "No bad publicity." That was his favorite mantra. There were the middle of the night emergency room visits and clandestine transfers of battered boys, spirited away by ambulance with the sirens off. Pila had witnessed much during her Rasta years at Linwood. Pila had finally come to the conclusion that Rasta was resistant to help. Medication, therapy, counseling, solitary confinement, nothing worked. They had exhausted Linwood's entire field of expertise. Pila had even swallowed her pride and asked for help from her colleagues. Doctor Maynard had quickly put an end to that. Fuming, Pila gritted her teeth at the latest memo from the director. In just two short weeks he wrote, Rasta Jones would be twenty one years old and would be released to his own recognizance. What was he stuck on stupid? She would fight this. There had to be a way to keep Rasta institutionalized. Science was making some incredible breakthroughs every day helping doctors to understand the complexities of the mind. One day there would be help for someone like Rasta, Pila believed it with all her heart. Turning to her computer she began to compose a reply to Doctor Maynard. Two return responses were delivered to Pila's office on the twenty first birthday of Rasta Jones. One was a copy of Rasta's release form and the other was an order of immediate termination of Doctor Pila Thomas for gross insubordination. Pila did not know whether to be furious or afraid. She knew deep down in her heart though, that this would not be the last that they would hear from Mr. Jones. Looking helplessly at her miniature Hindu statue she screeched in frustration…"Help us all."

Rasta Jones, to his malevolent delight was inflicted on an unsuspecting populace. He was free. He had unwillingly come to Linwood as an angry boy, and now he was leaving the facility as a blight waiting to land with both feet, on a ripe society. Doctor Thomas made a vow to herself that she would keep up with all of the latest studies on treating mental illnesses in the criminally insane. For many years Pila had kept a written history on Rasta Jones. She compiled quite a large dossier, which contained news paper articles, police reports, extensive arrest reports for drugs, battery, robbery, rape, and suspected murder. She kept these in her locked drawer along with her illegally copied files from Linwood. It was all here, and it was incredible. Much of these facts about Rasta kept Pila up at night and convinced her to invest in an expensive alarm system as well as a small caliber hand gun. Rasta continued to wreak havoc and Pila patiently waited for their paths to cross again one day. They would meet again… in a way that would shake everything that Pila had ever believed.

Chapter 3
'The Valley Of Shadows'

The frantic call came in around four a.m. The shrill music to pop goes the weasel, shattered, what was a peaceful sleep for Katrina Martinez. Anzel had been in the too frequent throes of his baffling nightmares. Blindly reaching for the emergency cell phone issued from his employment as Chaplain at Bayridge Correctional Facility, he misjudged the distance and sent it flying across the room. Biting back a few choice words Anzel glanced guiltily at Katrina's curious face. Leaping out of bed he quickly recovered his phone and snapped, "What is it?" The agitated voice of his assistant Chaplain, Cleet Brown rushed into his ear. "Sorry for the early call Anzel, but we have a situation here. Can you get here a.s.a.p.? The large and in charge folks have got their knickers in a knot. Here's the low down, during the three days you were off." "Ahem." Anzel cleared his throat. "You mean my much needed vacation?" "Okay man, your vay cay, we received an inmate from upstate New York. He is violent, volatile and HIV Positive. Makes for a very bad combination, you agree?" "Uh huh" Anzel responded warily. "But what does any of this have to do with me hombre? It's four o'clock in the morning for crying out loud." Responding a little irritably himself Cleet countered with, "It does involve you in this way, after a violent episode in the holding cell around two a.m., this prisoner had to be forcibly contained by at least six officers. Man you wouldn't believe this dude's strength. He can't weigh more than a hundred and a quarter soaking wet. Anyway, after they had him jacketed and calmed down, he started demanding to see you." "What do you mean see me?" "Anzel, just get here man, they're wanting some answers from you, okay? Off the record, cover yourself in the blood and bring some blessed oil and some word with you, this is the real deal bro. Bye." Anzel nodded numbly at the dial tone as his stomach rolled with an unnamed dread. He had a bad feeling that this situation had something to do with the dreams he had been having. Something about the questions he had to ask himself tickled his brain, *"Who was this stranger and what does he want from me?"*…He continued to stare at his cell phone as if it had the answers.

Fully dressed now, Anzel could not stop the tremors racing up and down his spine. Even when Katrina rubbed his back and softly prayed in his ear he continued to shake. Usually when Katrina quoted the Twenty Third Psalm in Spanish, it would make Anzel's eyes twinkle, but this morning it felt too much like a warning. Something about the words, "Valley of the shadow of death", whispered along the edges of his subconscious. "Lord, what is this?" He prayed. "I feel as though I'm going into something very dark." Still fretting, Anzel kissed Katrina's worried lips goodbye and got behind the wheel of his car and nervously backed out of the garage. Anzel's prayers were broken and distracted as he took the thirty minute drive to Bayridge. As Anzel pulled into his assigned parking space he felt another tremor pass through his body. How could someone he's never met have this effect on him? This was insane. During his more than eight years as Chaplain at Bayridge, he had looked upon the faces of pure evil more times than he could count. Collecting himself, he bowed his head and prayed, "For God has not given me the spirit of fear, but of power, love and a sound mind." This prayer was as used by and comfortable to him as his favorite pair of wool socks. He definitely was not underestimating the raw power of these words. He had slain his share of dragons with these very words. He could almost imagine his beloved Katrina adding, "Amen, man of God." Stepping out of his car and facing the dark, ominous building, Anzel squared his shoulders and took a deep breath. After making a quick call to Katrina to let her know he had safely arrived, he turned his cell phone off and hurried through the personnel entrance...A new day, a new dragon.

Chapter 4

'The Man in the Mirror'

Anzel was pleasantly surprised when a new officer he'd never seen before did not confiscate his small bottle of blessed oil. Everything was considered contraband. Instead, with a severe expression he gave Anzel a quick wink of approval. Puzzled, Anzel felt every feeling of fear and anxiety leave his body to be replaced with a....well a.....blanket of peace. Who was this new officer? He'd never seen him before but felt a powerful sense of.....familiarity with him. "Snap out of it Anzel." He chided himself. "You are losing it." This whole morning was beginning to take on a dreamlike quality. Just then the officer looked up from scanning the next person's belongings and caught Anzel's eyes. Holding up two fingers, he gave Anzel the universal sign for peace. Before Anzel could respond, the officer turned back to the scanner. Shaking his head as though to knock free some cobwebs, Anzel turned just in time to be met by Cleet Brown and two very aggravated looking corrections officers. Chaplain Martinez, you know officers Bailey and Alvarez. They all nodded towards each other as they started walking. Turning to Anzel, Cleet spoke in a low voice, "I'll fill you in on recent developments. Since I've spoken to you approximately ninety minutes ago the inmate decided to take a bite out of one of the officers and had to be muzzled. He will be transported directly to solitary as soon as you have talked with him. He keeps insisting that he has a personal message for you. Chaplain Martinez, did you hear me? Are you alright?" Everything around Anzel became muffled because he was staring down the corridor at the numbers on the infirmary door. He had never noticed the two numbers until now, six and zero. Anzel took a quick peek at his feet to see if his shoes had changed to wing tips. Anzel had prayed for the sick and dying many times in this infirmary, but an icy chill swirled all around him now. Was this the door in his dreams? What was behind the door? Cleet's voice moved him out of his thoughts and into motion. "We've got to get in there." Anzel's cheeks flushed slightly at the curious looks he was getting from the two officers. Were the numbers six and zero, a coincidence? He doubted it. Lord, what are you doing? Feeling a quickening in his spirit he turned to Cleet and said, "I feel a need to cover our group with prayer. Is that alright with you gentlemen?" The officers looked at each other and shrugged as Cleet nodded yes. When Anzel finished praying he looked up to see Cleet wiping a few stray tears. Suddenly, a loud bellow came from inside the infirmary. Officer bailey put a hand on Anzel's arm to get his attention. "Sir we need to finish briefing you on the prisoner before you enter the sick bay. The inmate in there is named Rasta Jones. He is thirty seven years old. He is HIV Positive. He is without any doubt one of the most dangerous, unpredictable inmates to ever occupy Bayridge. His history at his previous institution, Felton State Penitentiary is filled with violence and criminal activity. There is suspicion of three unsolved murders, one unsolved suicide, and at least four cases of arson. All implications point to inmate Rasta Jones. Anzel had turned a sickly shade of gray at the mention of Rasta's name. It had to be him. There couldn't be two of them. "Anzel, do you know this man?" Cleet asked carefully. Anzel gave him a distracted nod and continued towards the door. Perplexed, he had no choice but to follow. They were both overtaken by the officers before they reached the infirmary door. Officer Alvarez motioned for Anzel and Cleet to stand back from the door as it was activated from the main control panel by the officer completely encased in a protective glass. The sound of the lock being disengaged sent Anzel's pulse racing. He saw Cleet's mouth moving but he couldn't understand his words because he had just crossed the threshold from reality to nightmare, from sanity to madness. He stared open mouthed at the face from his nightmares. His eyes bugged at the wild, filthy mane of red hair and the pale translucent eyes. He couldn't see the mouth because of the muzzle, but he knew it would be curved into a cruel smile. The only things missing were the two horns protruding from his head. Anzel had no doubt that Rasta had horns, right where his heart should have been. Officer Alvarez carefully released the muzzle from the shackled and jacketed, Rasta. "No, don't remove his muzzle!" He tried to say but he felt his insides seize up. His belly clenched and erupted even as he fled the room followed by Rasta's shrieking laughter. As he stood in the corridor puking out his insides out on the severely buffed floor, the stunned faces of Cleet and the two officers turned him beet red with shame. To make matters worse, he was in earshot of Rasta's cruel laughter and bizarre statements. "Welcome home blood brother. We have missed you, yes we have summoned you. You have our mark and now we will claim our right to you." Rasta, laughed and laughed as Anzel helplessly retched and stared at the raised scar on his right forearm. The scar was in the shape of teeth marks.... human teeth marks. Remembering the circumstances behind the mark...his insides shifted and spewed out his humiliation onto the shoes of Cleet and the two officers.

Wearily, Anzel studied his haggard face in the personnel only bathroom with the lock safely in place. What just happened in there? He couldn't choose which was worse, the crazy things that Rasta was saying or his humiliating weakness in front of his coworkers. Squeezing the sides of his head he tried to forcefully erase his past memories of his encounter with Rasta Jones. He covered his mouth in time to stop the whimper that tried to escape. He had fervently hoped that Rasta had died or had fallen off the earth years ago, and now here he was, back, as large as life, to pick right up where he left off. Running a trembling hand over his face Anzel jerked his head back as it hit him. That monster in his dreams was Rasta. But how was it possible? Okay God what's going on here? Anzel almost jumped out of his skin as an urgent knock sounded on the door. "Chaplain Martinez, Anzel, are you alright? Do you need me to call your wife or someone?" "No, no, don't do that, she'll just worry." Sighing with frustration, he winced as he heard the tremor in his own voice. Clearing his throat he continued, "Thanks for looking out for me, but I'll be fine, just give me a few more minutes." He heard the muffled sounds of Cleet speaking to someone as he moved away from the door. Turning on the cold water Anzel attacked his face until every trace of his tears were gone. Feeling more in control he opened the door and stepped outside instantly relieved that there was no one in sight. Suffering the excruciatingly slow checkout process to exit the prison, Anzel found that he could not make eye contact with anyone. Walking to his car, he searched his memory for any verse from the bible that could help him make sense of all of this. Suddenly, Katrina's sweet voice praying the ninety first Psalms came to light in his mind. *"He who dwells in the secret place of The Most High, shall abide under the shadow of The Almighty. I will say of The Lord, He is my rock, my fortress, My God, in Him will I trust."* Anzel noticed that his hands were no longer trembling as he started the car. He replayed what happened over and over again on the ride home. Yes Katrina would help him figure out this nightmare come to life. She would hold him and stroke his head and everything would be alright, just like always. Right? But somehow he knew, it wouldn't be alright, it would never be alright again… Because nightmares really do come true sometimes.

Chapter 5

'Ready or Not, Here I Come'

When Anzel pulled into the garage he noticed his pastor's car was parked on the street. He was just muttering his disappointment when the front door opened and Katrina and the twins ran outside and leapt upon him. Holding him tightly from all sides, Katrina covered him with kisses as his girls showered him with giggles. All Anzel could do was laugh as he asked, "Who are you people? Do I know you?" "Silly Daddy," the girls said simultaneously. Cupping Anzel's face tightly Katrina searched his eyes. Anzel's bottom lip trembled slightly and Katrina's eyes clouded over in alarm. She started to say something but clamped her lips together as she glanced at the twins. Putting on a brave smile she said, "C'mon into the house sweetie, girls let daddy walk, you have to let go of his legs." Grabbing Anzel's hand Katrina whispered, "Baby, Cleet called me and told me a little bit of what happened. I didn't know what else to do, I was so worried. I hope you don't mind, I called Pastor Lockhart. I know how you feel about our privacy, but you have to agree, we need help with this... this...whatever it is. Pastor promised he would be here only to listen and to pray." Looking at the raw love and compassion in his wife's eyes almost made him break down again, right in the garage. He allowed Katrina to lead him into the house like a little child. He was so tired, the vivid nightmares, and now this...but what exactly was this?

Katrina waved goodbye to her mom as she drove away with an excited pair of twin grand girls. They were going out with grandma for a day of shopping that would end with a drive through visit to Rudy Burgers. True to his promise Pastor Dijin Lockhart sat quietly, with his head bowed for forty five minutes while Anzel battled with his resurfacing memories, along with his need for confession to his wife. Katrina sat at Anzel's feet heavily cloaked with fear of the unknown to come. She was determined to face anything that affected her family, head on. Silently she sat and watched the battle rage in Anzel's handsome face and she felt every bit of his pain. "Relief Lord." She silently pleaded. Both Pastor Dijin and Katrina startled when Anzel's voice broke the heavy silence. "I'm ready to talk about it now. Katrina, Pastor, I have a story to tell. It's not an easy story, but it's true. It's about one year out of my life. A year that I have buried so deep, that even I have trouble believing it really happened. Katrina, baby, I need you to understand, that when I first met you when we were just kids, my family was moving away from an old life. We were hoping to forget the past and begin fresh. I was twelve years old when we moved into your neighborhood. I was small for my age and I hated it. My Father and Mother were very private people, and what went on in the Martinez household, good or bad, stayed there." Anzel rubbed his face and groaned. "This is very hard for me to talk about, you understand pastor?" Dijin gave him a nod of encouragement. Anzel looked expectantly at Katrina who smiled and reached over and gave his hand a light squeeze. He continued in a more confident tone, "About a month after my tenth birthday my parents started going through a rough period. There was a lot of fighting, screaming and breaking of dishes." Anzel smiled and tossed a tease at Katrina, "Mama was a hot tamale just like you, eh chicka?" Katrina threw a pillow at his head, which he easily dodged. With a soft expression on his face he said, "Seriously Katrina, you remind me a lot of my mom. She was fierce when it came to loving the Lord and her family. She was so strong and she had a lot of passion, which she was very verbal about. Even in the storms, she did what she had to do. Don't get me wrong, I saw mama cry many a night, but she would always say to us kids, "Whatever you build, if it's family, friendships, jobs or anything else, you better build it on The Rock of Salvation." "I must have heard that a thousand times in my life. Anyway, one day my dad decided to sow his oats and he packed up his clothes and moved out and left us, just like that. No explanation. Mama was devastated. Thank God that didn't stop mama from doing what she had to do, she got up and went to work. Unfortunately that pretty much left us six kids without supervision. Being the youngest I was left to amuse myself most of the time. My amusement being, learning to smoke cigarettes and marijuana. I learned to drink until I passed out and of course, my introduction to pornography. Mama discovered what was happening to her family, but how was she to stop us? Many a night I would hear her prayers to God, but I didn't know God, not really. Mama took us to church every Sunday without fail, but we never paid much attention to the preacher." Katrina noticed that Anzel's accent had gotten thicker as he reminisced about the past. "I hated my father at that time and for a long time after he returned home. With anger and unforgiveness at my broken security, rebellion was my natural course. So my third appearance before a judge at the tender age of eleven years and two days, landed me in the Linwood Facility for Boys. My sentence was for one year, but it may as well have been for life. Man oh man, mama howled like they had given me a life sentence or the death penalty. I'm so ashamed of the cruel way I rejected my family back then. I blamed my parents for splitting up and my siblings for not getting caught. I even blamed God in a way, I think. I wouldn't even receive visits from mama, and of course my father never tried to see me." Anzel began wringing his hands and Katrina sat up because she knew he only did that when he was deeply distressed. She scooted closer and rested her hand on his knee. He stilled his hands and visibly relaxed, which made her relax. He started again slowly, "Being small for my age sometimes had its advantages, but not in this case. I mean I wasn't a punk, I was small but I was a scrapper, but I quickly found out that my kind of tough was nothing in a place like that. My third week there, the after light out beatings were a nightly ritual. The average inmate there was the typical cold hearted bully as on the outside. Two months in and they lost interest in me and concentrated on the newer arrivals. Three boys came in the new shipment. A puny Caucasian boy named Wesley, a hard looking older Oriental boy named Kabuki, and lastly and most importantly a small, mixed boy with wild red hair and soulless pale blue eyes." Anzel shuddered as he said the boy's name. "Rasta Jones." Katrina gasped, and Dijin pursed his lips and whistled softly. Anzel continued in a deadpan voice. "Rasta was about my height and build, and we shared the exact same birthday. That really freaked me out. Rasta had the coldest stare I had ever seen. Even when the older boys beat him to a pulp, Rasta never, ever cried. He always had this weird little smile on his lips. He never even lost that grin when big Jonas broke his arm in three places. Afterwards the boys labeled Rasta as loco and started to avoid him. They went after the new recruits coming in. That's when Rasta turned the tables on them. It was strange, but it's almost like Rasta used all of the pain that was inflicted on him to grow with, if that makes any sense. It made him more fearless, more powerful." Pastor Dijin had not interrupted, but he was looking intently at Anzel and hanging onto his every word. "Even with the cast on his arm he became something to contend with. Things started happening at Linwood that were out of the norm. The staff's personal belongings began to disappear. There was an increase in vandalism. There were small acts of arson, along with the discovery of dead animals along the edges of the property. Animals with the blood drained out of them, mutilated. Rasta got high on fear, you could see pure pleasure in his eyes...and his laughter...so weird. His favorite pastime was terrorizing or hurting someone and making them beg for mercy. I did my share of begging, we all did, and of course none was forthcoming. Mostly though, we tried to stay out of his line of vision. On this particular day about eleven months into my sentence", Anzel grabbed his head in both hands as the memories came freely now, making their own pace. "It was a Wednesday, cream style corn day. We all knew how much Rasta loved cream style corn. We used to secretly laugh about it. I hate that stuff to this day. This unfortunate day, we were the targets of Rasta and his flunkie's food extortion. The lunchroom officer had just moved to the far side of the room and had his back turned, deeply in conversation with another guard. Rasta and his bloodhounds plopped down at the quickly vacated table right next to ours. Our pitiful little group consisted of Wesley, me, and two other boys. We already knew the drill. You don't ask any questions or make any comment, or do anything that will draw attention. You just hand over whatever was demanded of you and count yourself lucky that you didn't get hurt...this time. Rasta demanded our corn, which we expected...little Wesley said no....totally unexpected. In a tiny, trembling voice he said "no...I...I...want my corn today." Everyone within earshot froze. My eyes shot to Rasta's face, and then to his posse, and then back to poor Wesley. Rasta never said a word in response, and that more than anything else, along with his grin, unnerved us." Anzel shuddered at the vivid memory. Continuing in a slightly lower tone he said, "Rasta stood up and nodded to his buddies, then pointed his finger at Wesley like it was an imaginary gun, and pulled the trigger. Wesley looked like he had seen a ghost. Needles to say we had all lost our appetites by then. Leaning against the wall near the door waiting to be released, Rasta stared unflinchingly at Wesley with that scary smile on his mouth until it was time to go. Before he disappeared through the door he gave Wesley a chilling wink. We were all looking at poor Wesley, some with pity, some with scorn...and most with relief that it was him and not us.

Anzel began shivering so hard that Katrina jumped up and hurried into their bedroom to get their heavy comforter. She wrapped it snugly around him and he looked up and gave her a grateful smile. Pastor Dijin spoke up now, "Katrina will you go and make a pot of strong black coffee for us? Anzel, just relax for a few minutes and regroup while I pray for you, is that okay?" Through his chattering teeth Anzel said, "No offense pastor but I like my coffee just like Katrina, smooth and brown with plenty of sweet." He tried to get his lips to form an answering smile to Dijin's chuckle, but they were trembling too much. Abruptly, Dijin bowed his head and began to pray. "Heavenly Father, we commit our hearts and minds into Your merciful care. You have made a promise to us that no weapon formed against us shall prosper, and that there is nothing too hard for You. We rest in knowing that You will never put more on us than we can bear. Hold onto Your faithful son, Anzel as he walks through this difficult memory and remind him that You have removed him out of harm's way for such a time as this. We pray for the peace that surpasses all understanding with our hearts and minds stayed on You. I feel a breakthrough coming Lord, of deliverance for Anzel, from these crippling dreams and paralyzing fear. We decree the victory today in Jesus name Amen." Katrina echoed a hearty "Amen!" from the kitchen. After draining his second cup of coffee, Anzel said, "Okay, Katrina, pastor, let's do this. I need to get this stuff out and hopefully be done with it. I really had this stuff buried deep. Alright here goes, poor little Wesley never stood a chance after that. Rasta had a new hobby…Wesley. He unleashed a campaign of terror against that boy, you wouldn't believe. Man, they played with him like a cat playing with a mouse, until he tires of it and kills it. They stole everything he had of value. They vandalized his schoolwork and books, and they wrote obscene things about him on the bathroom walls, but this is a little bit of the worst, they put dead animal parts and feces in his bunk. Wesley tried to get help, but you know how it is, the more he complained, the worse it got for him. They seriously laid into that poor kid. I believe the staff was just as scared of Rasta as the inmates were. Except for one

little psychiatrist, who worked with us. I overheard her tell
Rasta one time, that he did not run her or her office. She told
him she wasn't moved by his staring or his threats, but that she
would get him the help he needed, because he surely needed a
lot of help. Rasta just laughed in her face and walked away.
Poor Wesley's days were numbered for some serious hurt. The
attacks had become unbearable for Wesley and he was at his
breaking point." Anzel started wringing his hands again.
Katrina started to reach out to him but a sharp nod from Dijin
stayed her hands. "Now we're coming to the worst of it. It was
a Saturday night, following a pretty quiet day. There was only
one officer on shift, which was usual. I remember there was a
strange feeling in the air all that day. It felt like it was charged
with …I want to say danger, but I was just a kid, so I'm remembering from a child's perspective, you see?" Katrina and
Dijin nodded in unison. "We were all very skittish, since
Wesley had gotten the news that he would be going home that
Monday morning. Wesley was so relieved to be getting away
from his abusers. Maybe that's why he got a little careless on
that night. I never understood why he didn't stay close to his
bunkmates. Around forty five minutes to lights out, Wesley
went missing. We didn't dare ask anyone in authority for help,
because we didn't want to do anything to jeopardize his leaving Linwood. Something didn't smell right about the whole
thing though. For some reason I was elected to search for
Wesley. Ole wimpy Pete was the officer on duty that night and
it was always a piece of cake to get past him. All he cared about
was sleeping behind the glass barrier. Once I'd gotten past the
unmanned monitor a wave of fear washed over me. What was
I scared of? There was just such weirdness in the air. I was one

nervous little Chico. I was some hero huh? What was I going to do against the hardest criminals at Linwood? The odd thing was that I knew exactly where to look for Wesley. Heading to the showers I heard Wesley cry out and then it was cut off, you know like somebody put their hand over his mouth. He must have gotten loose because then he said, "Stop, leave me alone, I promise I won't tell!" I could tell he was crying. "Please Rasta, why are you doing this?" Then he screamed. I held my breath and tiptoed to the door. My heart was pounding so hard I was afraid they would hear it. I pushed open the door and was greeted by a sight so unreal, I don't know if I can get you to picture this, but I'll try my best. Wesley was lying on the floor, completely naked, covered from head to toe with bite marks oozing blood. They were holding him down and feeding on him like a pack of hellish dogs. Mercifully Wesley had fainted. Only now, those demon possessed eyes turned towards me. Before I could will my feet to run, they were on me clawing, ripping and tearing at my clothes. Some of them were laughing but Rasta was growling like an animal. I don't think I've ever been that scared in my life. I really freaked out when I saw the deep, ugly bite marks on Wesley's neck. It was every vampire movie that I had ever seen rolled into one. These days they try to glamorize vampirism, but the truth of the matter is that spilled blood has a heavy coppery smell, a sickening cloying scent, and there was so much of it. There was a palpable feel of evil all around us. Cold, frigid air surrounded our group on the floor, making Rasta's wicked laughter swirl around his face. They were enjoying my fear so much that they forgot to cover my mouth, and when I realized it, I yelled as loud as I could. Something heavy landed on my head and I must have blacked out." Anzels teeth were chattering again. Alarmed by what she was hearing Katrina rose and wrapped her arms tightly around Anzel's shoulders. Anzel kept talking through his shivering teeth. "It was horrible. There was Wesley, unconscious, with so much blood loss and them holding me down and Rasta leaning over me with a bloody, dripping, grinning mouth. Staring into those unfeeling, eyes, I watched as a strange light glowed in them, then with a low, guttural voice, he threatened, "If you ever tell anybody that we did this to you and Wesley, I will find you wherever you try to hide in this world. I will find you and cut your heart out, and while it is still beating in my bloody hands, I will eat it and drink your blood. Believe it!" "Then Rasta, leaned his filthy, bloodstained mouth over my right forearm and sank his teeth into it. He howled with laughter and said, "We are blood brothers and now nothing will ever separate us." Even in shock and the terrible pain in my arm I felt this strange disquiet in my heart. I think Rasta felt it too because he gave me this odd look, almost like he was afraid of me or something. Then he covered it up by shoving me away and telling his cronies to let me and Wesley go. Before he turned completely away though, I saw a look of disgust on his face. One of his gang looked like he was going to protest but when Rasta faced us again, that cold, dead glare was back in place, and the protest died on the boy's lips." Turning to Katrina Anzel asked, "Babe, remember I told you I had been bitten by a dog? That bite was Rasta's permanent reminder to keep my mouth shut." Giving Pastor Lockhart a stricken look, he continued with difficulty. "Maybe if I had said something sooner someone could have stopped him, but I was so scared and ashamed because I had wet myself and they were laughing about it." Dijin was standing over Anzel now with his hand on his shoulder. "Anzel, you're being too hard on yourself. You were just a little boy, who was confronted with an evil that you had no understanding of." Anzel shook his head rapidly in agreement. "I just have a little more to add. Everything was kept hush hush as usual and Wesley was patched up and shipped off home without being able to say goodbye to anyone. Then I received an early release about two weeks later, but it was months before I could sleep through a whole night. My parents didn't know how to deal with this kind of situation and the therapists that worked for the state weren't interested enough, so it was easier to just bury it and pretend it never happened. That's why, when I saw Rasta today at the prison." Katrina interrupted, "So you really saw him? You saw the real Rasta? Cleet didn't give me all of the details." Anzel continued as if he didn't hear her. "All that fear and revulsion came back, all those buried memories. The boogey man in living color. Now the dreams are beginning to make some sense, but I still don't get the part with the mirror." Pastor Dijin looked at Katrina curiously, but she didn't take her eyes off of Anzel. Suddenly Anzel jumped up and started pacing back and forth. Stopping in front of Dijin he said, "The presence of evil in that infirmary today was so strong pastor, it made me violently sick." Dijin was roughly worrying the cowlick on top of his head, which was an indication that he was weighing his words carefully. "Son, you have to tell me about these dreams. No more holding back. I sense that the Lord is in on this but I need to have all of the facts so that I can know what my part in it is." With a sharp clap of his hands, startling Anzel and Katrina, Dijin excused himself and telephoned home to tell Ella not to wait dinner for him. Following suit, Katrina phoned her mom and made her a very happy grandmother by asking her to keep the girls overnight. Shaking off a feeling of dread, she assured her mom everything was alright. Pasting on a bright smile she rejoined Anzel and Dijin. He was just beginning the difficult task of explaining his nightmares as Dijin listened with widened eyes. When Anzel ran out of words, he sighed with exhaustion. Dijin signaled him and Katrina to join him on his knees in the middle of the floor. He began his prayer in his typical manner, "Heavenly Father, we three, your faithful servants, prostrate our earthly forms in your presence, asking for your forgiveness of any sins that stand between us and an answer to our petitions. Tonight Lord we are asking for understanding of the path you have chosen for us. We know that you have not given us a spirit of fear, but of power, love, and a sound mind. We also understand that the enemy has some power, but you have all power. Nothing can be done to your servants except you allow it. Father if this is a journey that only Anzel can travel, give us the leading that we need to assist him in every way. Cause Anzel to know that wherever You may carry him, he will not be alone." At those words, Katrina looked up with a sharp intake of breath. Pastor Dijin squeezed her hand and kept praying. "Jesus we trust You with our very lives, and offer our whole selves for Your service. In all things we pray that You are glorified." With a troubled glance at Anzel, Dijin finished with, "let Your will be done in the precious name of Jesus, Amen." The three agreed with an extra "Amen," and the room was thick with the presence of God, so much so that for the next thirty minutes, no one spoke a word or moved from their prostrate positions. When the glory cloud lifted enough for them to utter a sentence, Dijin opened his bible and began to read from 2 Corinthians, chapter ten, verses three, four and five. When he finished, he spoke with a supernatural authority to Anzel. "Study these scriptures on spiritual warfare and protection and also Ephesians chapter six and Psalm ninety one. You have to learn to fight the enemy on his own turf. The victory is already yours, but you have to go through this, it's all in God's plan. For Rasta as well as you, it is *The Thinning*." Suddenly the power seemed to drain out of Dijin leaving him looking dazed and frail. He shook his head as if to clear it, seemingly unaware that Anzel had grabbed his arm in excitement. "But why me? What does God want from me? What is the Thinning? Pastor please!" Katrina began reciting the twenty third Psalms in Spanish with as much passion as Anzel had ever heard from her. He stared at her with dull eyes. Gone was the comfort and pride he'd always felt to hear her struggling with her broken Spanish. Now he only felt cold, alone and scared. He absently fingered the raised scar on his forearm. Three nights later Anzel began the habit of walking around their patio late at night, talking to The Lord. If he noticed the neighbor's curiosity he gave no sign of it. The dreams had returned with a vengeance, propelling him into these nightly vigils, because this time the image in the mirror had blood running from his mouth, and with burning, red eyes boring into him said, "I AM YOU. YOU ARE ME. WE... ARE...ONE!" Then the image shrieked with laughter as Anzel tore himself away in slow motion, yelling, "NOOOOOO!" Then he was falling into a dark pit, down and down he fell, gripped with mute terror. Just before impact he woke up in a cold sweat. Then he screamed, shocking Katrina awake and causing the neighbor's dog to bark...because the face looking back at him with cold dispassion from the mirror across the room was none other than Rasta Jones.

Doctor Pila Thomas smiled sweetly in her sleep, dreaming of her childhood in Sri Lanka, a small Island in North India. In her dream, she was chasing her older sister Ryia, whose name meant *singer*, through the tall rubber trees on their plantation. They were laughing so hard that Ryia was doubled over trying to get her breath. Suddenly she shot straight up and grabbed the front of her neck. Pila watched with wide eyes as Ryia's hands began to turn red. Making a horrible gurgling sound, she reached a small hand dripping with blood in Pila's direction. Her twelve year old eyes were round with surprise. Almost in slow motion, ten year old Pila watched her beloved sister topple backwards into a irrigation ditch directly behind her. Snapping awake, Pila realized that the whimpering sounds from her dreams were coming from her own throat. Sitting up, she gathered her blanket around herself, fretting over the dream. Raising a cold trembling hand to her forehead she questioned herself, why now after all of these years? So many years and so many miles ago that Ryia was killed by that stray bullet right before her eyes. The bullet, they later found out had come from the gun of a Tamil Rebel. It's strange, Pila mused, that even though the times were bloody and frightening due to the civil war, they still answered the timeless call of child's play. It would be ten years after her sister's death that their President Premdossa, would be assassinated by the same group of rebels. Thankfully Pila's parents had the foresight to send her to the United States to live with a distant cousin, before they too were killed in a car accident caused by a purposely blown out bridge. The eighteen years of civil war would claim the lives of more than sixty four thousand citizens, mainly civilians. Pila left her home and family, never to return. She was barely eleven years old. Now here she was returning there in her dreams. How was it possible? Her earliest memories of childhood were filled with lush trees and the fragrant, heady scent of tea leaves, with their strong herbal flavor. She shivered as she was pierced with a bitter sweet memory of her mother bending over her cook pot stirring rice and curry. Dried fish and fresh mangoes were also their main staples. It amused Pila that even now forty years later, she still liked to sit on the floor and eat hot curry and rice. Of course she got her curry from the fast food take out downtown, but it quenched a tiny bit of home sickness. So with one small travel bag, Pila Ahimsa, surviving child of Hindu parents came to live in the home of distant Christian cousins. It was quite a culture shock to her rigid Hindu upbringing. Unfortunately, what she was exposed to in her new home and odd little brick church was hypocrisy, legalism and prejudice. One exception stood out in Pila's memory. There was a tiny Caucasian Sunday school teacher, whom everyone but Pila called Mother Lou. Very uncomfortable because of her cultural differences, she refused to show her that much familiarity and called her Miss Lou instead. Miss Lou's patience and genuine love towards Pila almost convinced her that Jesus was real…almost. Pila did admire the peace that always seemed to accompany the woman like a cloud of perfume. It was always present when Miss Lou tried to share her peculiar beliefs. Thinking of Miss Lou gave Pila a concentrated curiosity…that helped lull her back to sleep.

Pila awoke to the ringing of her cell phone. Groggily she

slapped at it several times before her hand would obey the curl command. "Yes, doctor Thomas here." Reaching for her glasses she managed to knock over a neglected vase of posies, splashing greenish brown water on her beloved Persian rug. Oh and of course her expensive vase shattered into a GA-zillion pieces. "Sorry", she mumbled sheepishly into the receiver as if the caller had witnessed her clumsiness. "Good morning Doctor Thomas, you don't know me, but my name is Clarence Cleet Brown. I am the assistant Chaplain at Bayridge Correctional Facility. I may be a little bit out of my jurisdiction, but I'm calling about an inmate, he is a double lifer. He's a very troubled, violent man, with strange delusions. You come with high recommendations in the field of Sociopathy. According to this inmate's history, he has not responded to any treatments, therapy or rehabilitation procedures. If anything he seems to be more resistant and defiant. His behavior can at best be described as animalistic." Pila's heart was in her throat as she clutched the phone in a sweaty palm. "Doctor Thomas, are you still there?" Said a very concerned voice. "Yes, yes, I'm still here Mr. Brown. Before you continue I must tell you that I already know of this prisoner, there can only be one like him, I hope. I have quite a large file compiled on him from his incarceration as a child to adulthood and beyond. Although I have not had any new information, I have closely followed the corrupt life of one Mr. Rasta Jones." Pila shuddered as she said his name out loud. "Whew!" "Doctor Thomas can you meet with me to go over these files, then you can have a short visit with Mr. Jones? Maybe you can shed some light on what we're dealing with here." "Chaplain Brown, let me check my calendar and I promise I'll get back to you at my earliest convenience."

Her earliest convenience turned out to be…one week, two days, three nightmares and one visit to her own therapist later.

Rasta Jones lay face down in his cell sweating profusely, with the voices ranting and raving and threatening him. Rasta curled up and began to whimper against the relentless attacks. Warnings careened around inside his skull like ping pong balls. "SOMEONE'S COMING!" They screeched in panic. "THEY WANT TO SEPARATE US FROM YOU! YOU BELONG TO US! MAKE THEM GO AWAY, OR WE WILL MAKE YOUR MIND HURT! HURT, HURT, HURT!" Rasta knew their kind of hurt and he would avoid it at all costs. Maybe he would just end it right now. He'd tried several times before, but it was as if he could not die. The voices assured him though that even in death he couldn't escape them. Rasta believed them. For Rasta Jones, there was no way out…ever. The voices began to torment him again, "HE'S COMING! NOOOOOO! THE LIGHT THAT KILLS! YOU MUST STOP HIM! YOU MUST KILL THE LIGHT!" Images filled Rasta's mind. Hideous pictures of what was in store for him. The cell block rang with his screams of terror…along with the vicious threats to shut him up from the other spooked inmates.

At the exact same moments that Rasta was being terrorized, Anzel wrestled with tormenting spirits in his sleep. Invisible hands grappled for purchase on his throat, cutting off his air supply. The words, "STAY OUT!" Screamed inside of his skull and shocked him awake. With the fading image of a terrified Rasta Jones imprinted on his eyelids, Anzel dry heaved, threatening to lose his dinner. Sitting up in bed, he put his forehead into his trembling hands. He sneaked a quick peek at Katrina who, thankfully didn't stir this time. The nightmares were taking their toll on her almost as much as they were on him. Anzel made a decision, he would tell Katrina first thing in the morning that he was putting an end to his stubbornness and would seek professional help. Things were steadily getting worse…and he couldn't explain, pray, or chase the horrible dreams away.

"Anzel man, I'm telling you the truth, Rasta Jones is asking to see you, by name." Cleet Brown was whispering into the receiver, nervously looking around to see if he was being overheard by anyone. "You know, I could lose my job over this Anzel, the big boss is having a conniption fit. He wants to know what your connection is to Rasta and if your position as head Chaplain, or the security of the prison is being compromised in any way." Instantly angry Anzel said, "Hold on Cleet, what are you saying? They are discounting my years of faithful service, putting my position in jeopardy because of the insane ramblings of an inmate?" Cleet whispered sharply, "I'm going to call you from my cell phone in approximately thirty minutes." He hung up before Anzel could respond. Grateful that Katrina had taken the girls shopping, Anzel waited anxiously for Cleet's call. He didn't think he had the strength to explain this newest development to his wife. Exactly thirty minutes later, Cleet called back speaking in a normal tone, "Hey Anzel, I was really nervous there, I need my job just as I'm sure you do. Anyway, they questioned Inmate Jones and they allowed me to observe, via surveillance room, since you're still technically out on vacation. It was really bizarre man. Rasta kept insisting that you and he were blood brothers and that you shared some big secret. Then he began to demand….I mean strongly demand to see you. He didn't use the words "I want to see him", he said "We are waiting for him to come home." Around about this time I could see that the Psychologist was filing him away as a nut case, but the director seemed somewhat skeptical, and as soon as they had removed Rasta, he asked his secretary to pull up your file and background checks." Anzel listened without interruption, barely breathing, gripped by a feeling of helplessness. "Anzel, are you still there? I'm sorry Anzel I tried to reason with Director Williams, but he was looking at me as if my file was next." In a hoarse whisper Anzel said, "Thanks Cleet, just pray for me as hard as you can." "Brother, tell me what's going...." But Anzel broke the connection. Cleet stared at the phone blankly for a minute...then he bowed his head and obeyed the man of God's cry for help.

Chapter 6

'Taking A Trip Down Memory Lane' (So Scared)

Across town Katrina sat trembling in Doctor Pila Thomas' office. "Anzel would have a fit if he knew that I went behind his back to get him some help. After he received that call from Chaplain Brown, I couldn't keep sitting by and watching my husband come apart at the seams. Anzel is barely eating, and he wakes up almost every night screaming. Lately he's up at all hours, afraid to go to sleep. Now he's added pacing back and forth across our patio until the wee hours of the morning." Pila couldn't help but stare at the tissue in Katrina's hands that was worried beyond recognition. Weighing her words carefully she said, "Mrs. Martinez, I can understand your concern for your husband, but I'm not getting a clear picture of how I can be of help. I know that Cleet Brown recommended me, why, I don't know...but." "Please, Doctor Thomas, I need to know what this inmate has against my husband. He seems to have some kind of demonic influence over him." Pila cleared her throat before answering to the rising agitation in Katrina's voice. "Frankly Mrs. Martinez, I don't believe in that sort of thing, but I can assure you that many of the children who were in contact with Mr. Jones suffered in one way or another. "I don't know what good it will do, but I'll make room in my schedule to see your husband. It's always so much busier around the holidays though. However, it will have to be after my visit with the inmate in question, one week from today." Katrina shot out of her seat, startling Pila, she clasped both of Pila's hands in hers. "Oh, thank you so much. I thank God for you." Pila pulled away feeling very uncomfortable. "That's not necessary. Call my secretary in a few days and confirm an appointment, goodbye now." Katrina was quickly ushered out the door and found herself looking at a smirking secretary. Okay, that was the easy part, she consoled herself weakly... now getting Anzel to agree to come was going to take some fancy footwork.

Doctor Thomas stood shivering as the metal detector swept over her slender form. The officer looked at her with a hint of suspicion in her eyes. Pila was too concerned with the upcoming meeting with Rasta Jones, to give it more than a twinge of irritation. She quickly swallowed the thought "Idiot." She gathered up her items as they came through the belt. Patting her nervous stomach she glanced at the women's restroom and decided to ignore her uneasy cramping. Looking up she saw an attractive black gentleman waving in her direction...unconsciously giving her hair a quick pat, she headed in his direction.

This was one of the few times in their marriage that Anzel was livid with Katrina. She watched, amazed at the veins standing out in his neck. "You had no right to go behind my back and tell some shrink my problems. You were way out of line chicka." *He didn't bother to tell Katrina that he had already made up his mind to seek help.* Anzel, furiously paced back and forth while Katrina sat speechless and guilty, her eyes pleading for understanding. She opened her mouth to apologize and before she could utter one word, the storm that was her husband blew over. Contritely, Anzel pulled Katrina to her feet and wrapped her tightly in his arms. He buried his face in her hair, taking in her familiar scent of honeysuckle shampoo. "Oh baby girl, me amour; I truly love that you love me so much, but we have to work together in this thing." Squeezing Katrina tighter, he lifted her off of her feet. Suddenly turning serious, he set her down. "I feel like I'm drowning in some dark cesspool and all around me people are yelling, "HOLD ON ANZEL, WE'RE RIGHT HERE BESIDES YOU! But in that darkness I can't feel or hear anybody. I can't even feel God. Katrina baby, I'm scared to death. I have never been so scared in my life." Katrina reached up and cupped Anzel's face, and as she wound her fingers tightly in his silken tresses, a thought came to her. She quickly rejected it as she studied Anzel's tearstained face. She was going to lose Anzel. No matter how hard they prayed, he no longer belonged to her and the girls. Groaning, she hugged Anzel and desperately pressed her lips to his, inhaling his scent as if to memorize it. Her tears mingled with his as the thought became a piercing arrow through her heart. The thing that hurt the most was that she was certain that God knew all about it. Swallowing bitterly, she thought, "After all, wasn't He God?...The Omnipotent One?

On the morning of Rasta's appointment with Doctor Thomas, the voices had blasted him out of a troubled sleep with fearful shrieks and threats. "THE WOMAN KNOWS YOU, THE WOMAN FEARS YOUR POWER! YOU MUST USE HER FEAR WE NEED HER FEAR TO SURVIVE! SHE PLAYS AN IMPORTANT PART IN HIS COMING. YOU MUST LURE THEM IN, OR WE WILL KILL YOU! WE WILL KILL YOU FOREVER, BUT YOU WILL NEVER DIE! YOU

WILL NEVER DIE!" Pulling his threadbare blanket around his shoulders, Rasta buried his head in his hands and moaned like a wounded animal. Images appeared in his mind, of the torments that awaited him someday. Rasta's heart seized in his frail chest for an impossibly, long moment. The pain was horrendous. When it seemed he would black out in relief, his heart muscles relaxed. The voices laughed with malicious glee. Rasta knew that there was no way out for him in this sorry life or the next. Who was there to help him? Who had he ever helped or shown mercy to? When he heard the pitiful pleas of his victims, didn't it make his heart rejoice? He knew with great certainty that there was a life beyond this one. It would be a life that would last forever and ever. The voices had spoken to him when he was just a child hiding out in the woods from his evil stepmother. The voices spit and seethed with scorn as they warned him about the Son of God. Then they would whisper seductively to him about their dwelling place of fire and fear and hopelessness. Rasta knew that he was choosing damnation even though he was only a child and the voices made the consequences of his decision clear to him from the start. He freely walked into hatred and darkness. He'd lived his life that way ever since. He landed in and out of one institution after another. Waxing worse and worse like a volcano waiting to erupt. Rasta, Practiced every type of abominable sin in the sight of God and man. The resume included, gross perversion, murder for hire and for personal enjoyment. One of his favorite practices was vampirism, not for the squeamish, but Rasta had managed to find others who enjoyed it as much as he did... almost. For a short while drug and human trafficking funded a lavish lifestyle, but Rasta's enjoyment of his own product caused a quick downfall. Nothing was too low or unspeakable for him to participate in. Now the joy ride was over for him. He was serving two life sentences, which was a joke because he was in the last stages of being HIV Positive. The upside to this was that his strain of pneumonia kept him pretty much isolated from the regular prison populace, because of the air born contagion. Better for them he sneered. Rasta also knew that the voices were toying with him and using him like they always have. He feared that one of these times when his heart seized up, they were going to carry out their threats and take him to that place of torment. A rare sense of regret filled the pit of his stomach, but it quickly died in the blackness of his heart. An odd memory rushed through the door of opportunity. A small, red headed boy kneeling at the side of a bed praying, "If I should die, before I wake, I pray You Lord, my soul to take." The memory was violently ripped away in a torrent of words and images so foul and filthy…that Rasta mercifully passed out for a few seconds from the intensity of the attack.

Pila, wearing an expensive linen pantsuit, in her favorite color green, sat nervously in the worn padded chair staring at the blasted shell of the man Rasta Jones. She noted to herself her appreciation for the bullet proof glass between them after all of these years. Although Rasta looked like a pitiful helpless man, he exuded a dark power that reached beyond the glass partition. He had a full head of filthy red dreadlocks. Fascinated, and scratching her own head absently, Pila wondered if he had head lice. Even though Rasta looked feeble enough to be in a hospital bed, Pila had enough experience to know that a mentally ill patient could exhibit super human strength when agitated. She felt curious but safe knowing that he would remain shackled for the entire interview. He was also wearing a mouth piece which would only be removed for his responses. Pila felt compassion for the poor officer in charge of Rasta's transport to and from his cell; he looked less certain of his safety. Rasta's history of biting caused the guard to keep one nervous hand near his stunning weapon. Pila knew that she would be dreaming about those hate filled orbs staring across the glass at her, for a long time to come. Facing this mad child turned mad man, Pila squared her small shoulders and said…"Alright Mr. Jones, let's begin.

Preparing herself for a barrage of verbal abuse, she instructed the officer to remove Rasta's mouth piece. She watched the officer hesitantly reach forward and quickly snatch the piece loose. Careful not to get his fingers too close, he kept his other hand armed. Rasta studied him as if he were trying to decide whether to spit on him or laugh at the fear in his eyes. Rasta dismissed him and returned his vicious stare to Pila. Without speaking, he studied her as if she were an insect on the end of his pin. Squirming in her seat and unconsciously clasping the collar of her crisp new jacket, Pila cleared her throat and began again, "Good morning Mr. Jones." She didn't wait for a response in these cases, and knowing what she knew about the prisoner already, she moved on quickly. "I understand that you have been having some distress in your cell at night, possibly some nightmares?" She had been staring at her paperwork through this entire exchange and now she chanced to glance up at him. She forced herself to look directly into his glacier like eyes. The intensity of his return look gripped Pila's heart because he was grinning at her like a rabid dog. The rest of Pila's comments died on her lips. Rasta apparently found this extremely funny and he roared with laughter. The officer took a reluctant step in Rasta's direction, but regaining her composure, Pila stopped him with a lifted hand. Rasta's mocking laughter broke the yoke of fear from Pila's tongue and she became all professionalism now. "Mr. Jones, please tell me about your dreams, I want to help you." For a fleeting second, his eyes seemed to reach out in a desperate plea; then, the icy glare returned. In a gravelly voice, Rasta spoke, "Miss Doctor, I got a question for you." The already cool temperature in the room plunged dramatically. Pila shook herself slightly amazed that she could faintly see her breath. Gooseflesh rose up and down her arms because right before her eyes Rasta's appearance began to alter. He became fuller in his facial features. Then his cheeks began to take on the rosy tint of a man in the best of health. Pila startled as the officer inched closer to the exit door, incredulous. Even though Pila had experienced this type of paranormal manifestation before, she was still spooked. One of her former colleagues, strong in her Christian beliefs, called this sort of thing, demonic possession, but of course Pila didn't believe in that superstitious nonsense, and she had let her know in no uncertain terms too. Rasta interrupted her thoughts, "Hey doc, why do you sit on the floor and eat your rice and curry sometimes?" This he said this with a sweet angelic look on his face. Pila's head jerked back in surprise. Before she could respond he said, "Do you still miss your sister, Ryia, our little songbird?" Now he was beginning to laugh. Pila was speechless. "What was it like doc, you know, watching Ryia twisting in that ditch with all that blood covering her clothes? I wish I had been there, I would have drunk her blood." Pila jumped up, toppling her chair backwards, and clutching her throat in horror. Rasta was bouncing up and down in his restraints, screaming with malicious, gleeful laughter. Pila was backed up against the far wall staring in shock at Rasta. The last thing that Rasta was able to say before the officer and his backup were upon him was, "Bring our brother. Bring us Anzel Martinez. Pila fled from the room sobbing, professional ethics forgotten. She was ten years old again…and she just wanted to run away from the boogey man.

Chapter 7
'Baby Steps'

Returning home early from her hair salon appointment, Katrina took off her coat and set her favorite rust colored Hobo bag on the floor near the front door. She hurriedly dialed Doctor Thomas's office. The recorded message played the same disappointing words. "Doctor Thomas is not in the office at this time, please try again later." Katrina threw the cell phone down in frustration. She ran her hands through her fresh salon hairdo. It fell in soft auburn waves across the top of her shoulders. She was too preoccupied to consider what Anzel's reaction would be to her new color and style. Why wouldn't somebody answer the phone at Doctor Thomas's office? She had been trying to get an appointment for her husband for two weeks now. She chewed furiously at a freshly manicured nail as these thoughts prickled in her mind. Thank God for doting grandparents. She had the house to herself until later this evening. Sighing heavily, she knelt and bowed her head. It took a few minutes for her words to come. "Lord, I don't know how much longer we can go on like this. Anzel is so exhausted. He can barely get any sleep without being haunted by those crazy dreams. Last night I found him curled up behind the clothes hamper in the laundry room. He was whimpering and shivering like a newborn puppy. He says that Rasta keeps calling to him, telling him to come home. But the most disturbing thing to me is that he feels very strongly that You are prompting him to go and see this man too. Lord I'm trying to be strong for my husband, but I need a sure word from You about how to proceed. So, what do we do Lord?" Bowing even lower, Katrina waited for an answer. The Lord remained silent on the matter. The only sounds came from the ticking of their antique grandfather clock in the foyer, and the breaking of Katrina's heart. Wearily she rose from her knees, located the local phone directory and looked up the home phone number of Doctor Pila Thomas. If she had to stake out somebody's house...Katrina was determined to get some results...today.

Snuggly wrapped in her green Chenille throw, Pila picked up the phone on its third chirp. Normally she didn't respond to unfamiliar numbers, and she'd forgotten to enlist her answering service but, something compelled her to take this call. "Hello?" Pila heard a tremendous sigh followed by near hysterical weeping. Fearing the worst she carefully asked, "Who's calling please?" Trying to stop the tears had now turned into hiccups, and Pila was able to barely make out a name. "Mrs. Martinez, why are you calling my home dear? Has something happened to your husband?" Calmer now Katrina spoke quickly, "Doctor Thomas, my husband is getting worse by the day. I have been calling your office for two weeks trying to get him in there. But all I've gotten is your answering machine." Pila could hear the accusation in her voice. "I must apologize to you Mrs. Martinez, but I've been....ill." She chose not to share the fact that the illness hadn't been completely physical. She had suffered a mild breakdown. Her therapist had ordered her on complete bed rest since her visit to the prison. This was the first day that she had felt like her old self again. "Oh Doctor Thomas, I'm so sorry!" Hearing the genuine concern in Katrina's voice warmed Pila's heart. "Please forgive me for intruding. Maybe I should have waited for you to return to your office." Knowing in her newly warmed heart that it was the right thing to do Pila said, "No, no Mrs. Martinez, I will meet with you and your husband on Tuesday morning at ten o'clock. Now please give me the name and phone number of your pharmacy and I will phone in a prescription for a sedative for your husband. Try to make sure he's well rested for our appointment." She jotted down the information and hung up. The phone call had two different effects. Oddly, Pila had a surge of exhilaration, sensing they were on the verge of a huge breakthrough that would solve the mystery that was Rasta Jones. While Katrina had an overwhelming feeling of dread that... she and Anzel were on the brink of a disaster from which they would never, ever, recover.

Anzel stared moodily out of the large picture windows of his and Katrina's home. They sparkled brightly from Katrina's recent polishing. He was further aggravated by the fact that she had laid out his least favorite rust colored shirt. "She must be annoyed with me," he thought sheepishly. He was feeling the crush of too many sleepless nights that tried to spin him into depression's provocative embrace. There he sat, completely untouched by the pre holiday snowflakes falling softly within his eyeshot. It was thirteen days before Thanksgiving which was always a big deal at the Martinez home. Katrina always went all out for the holidays, with vivid colors and lots of floral arrangements. He usually stepped out of her way and let his sweetheart work her magic. The result was, their home was usually magazine perfect for every holiday. Anzel really had to applaud his wife this year because with all of the drama going on in their lives, she didn't miss a beat with keeping the girls excited, even if he was the Grinch lately. When the girls became frightened by daddy's cries in the night, Katrina taught them to pray for daddy and plead the blood of Jesus over him. Anzel had to smile at the seriousness with which they took this to task. Man, he really loved his girls. He adored all three of them. Suddenly remembering why he was sitting in front of the crystal clear window erased the smile from his face. He didn't relish the idea of seeing Doctor Thomas, who would probe his brain, pouring more salt on his open memories. He had to do something though. His life was spiraling out of control, and yet he was positive that God was at the end of this thing. It was what he had to base all of his salvation on thus far. He knew that he belonged to God, and he had never had a reason to doubt it before. Did the *Thinning* have something to do with his personal faith in God? Anzel made his decision. No matter what his trials and testing would be, no matter what the cost, he would finish the course. The victory was already purchased by Jesus Christ…Now, if he could only hold onto to that thought during the terror of his of his dreams.

Chapter 8
'Sleep Walking Awake'

Pastor Dijin Lockhart stirred slightly on his favorite over-stuffed recliner. While he was taking his mid morning nap, he was in the throes of a vivid dream. He dreamed that he was a young man again, and he was running along a path that was filled with moving shadows. He could feel his perspiration cooling from a slight breeze. Ignoring the shadows, he hurried to reach his destination. Sensing that he'd been running a long time, he was mildly surprised to find that his breathing wasn't labored. The constantly changing path began to throw him off balance, because at some points it curved sharply, while at others it would slant downwards making him lightheaded. A wild overgrowth of trees made Dijin duck his head frequently. Bursting with an unusual sense of determination, he pressed on. On and on he jogged using youthful legs that never seemed to tire. Suddenly an intense driving need began to overtake his senses. He was listening for a voice. If he did not hear the sound of this voice, he felt he would surely die "No!" He cried as his legs began to feel the strain and his muscles cramped painfully. Through the haze of his pain Dijin realized that his own voice carried no sound. Suddenly, through the thick plant growth ahead he could make out the pin point of a stark white light. In his haste to reach that light, Dijin stumbled over a thick root and fell to his knees. Shaken, he began to crawl towards the light, ignoring his bleeding knees and palms.

Desperately reaching with both hands, he discovered that the light was coming from behind a thick wall made of some type of glass or crystal. Heartbroken Dijin leaned his face against it and beat his fist while he wailed unashamedly. His whole being craved the light and the voice. He knew in his dream heart that no matter what it took or how long, he would do whatever he needed to satisfy this need. And so he sobbed, and he pounded and wept and tapped....tapped. He awoke to a gentle tapping on his cheek. "Honey, what's wrong? You're crying Dijin, wake up." Ella's face came slowly into focus, with concern deeply etched into it. Dijin shook himself and sat up rubbing his teary eyes. "I'm alright Ella I was just having a dream. Will you get me a drink of cold water please? Man I'm thirsty." Finishing the cold, sweet water, he promised Ella he would fill her in before the day's end. Ella twisted her mouth at the brush off, but she let the matter rest and with a shake of her head, she left to go on her daily, two mile run. Dijin sat back in his chair and tried to recall the full dream. "Oh Lord, now I'm having dreams." He said wearily. Something was bugging him about the significant points in the dream. There was something he needed to remember. The glass wall and the bright light were triggering something in his memory. The thought teased the edges of his consciousness. Making his way into the kitchen he lifted out his lunch plate and thoughtfully chewed on his peanut butter and prune sandwich. It was one of his favorite mid day meals. He humorously dubbed it, *'The ties that un-bind'*. Ella had almost cracked her jawbone laughing the first time she heard it, but after the third and fourth time, she only sighed and rolled her eyes. Then, like a jolt of lightening, the reason for the nagging feeling in his memory became clear. It came with so much clarity that he dropped a big glob of prune spread down the front of his beat up old jersey. "Shoot!" He bellowed. His final term paper from his last year in Seminary. No wonder he had forgotten, it was years ago. Now the memories came flooding back. It took Dijin nine months to compile all the information and six weeks to manuscript it. The Uriankhai Monks. They were a bizarre sect of Siberian Monks who fled during the subjugation of the son of Genghis Khan, in the year twelve hundred and seven. Then less than eighty years later they were almost extinct. Hundreds of years after their extinction historians discovered puzzling artifacts that had managed to survive the years of nature and plunder. Once the door to his memory opened up, he was pulling up facts like a youngster. Later in eighteen hundred and three, a previously unknown archeologist of Russian descent, Sergey Lebedev, stumbled upon the ancient, crudely built, mock monastery. He had unwittingly dug up a very important piece of history. In Sergey's bumbling discovery, he'd uncovered the ancient forbidden practice of 'Prague Nuine'. It was a sacred practice of the Uriankhai Monks passed down in solemn ceremonies to each generation of hand chosen high priests and monks. Sometimes members of high political standing were allowed to place children in the monastery for training. The practice was abolished several years following the Mongolian invasion after a high official's first born son died during this practice. Two thirds of the monks were slaughtered, while the rest were driven into hiding. Interestingly enough though, the spiritual hold on the remaining monks, increased in its fervency. Dijin scrubbed at his forehead furiously as the story began to take shape in his mind. Each monk or priest was given his own solid block of crystallite. Then in a very special ceremony, he vowed to dedicate his entire physical life, and through every means he possessed, he would attempt to reach the jewel that was fused into the center of his crystallite. Their belief was that the jewel held the key to eternal life, and that only a few were worthy to breach the stone. They only ate and drank enough to sustain their lives for the task. Their whole focus was...Dijin's eyes widened. Their whole purpose was, oh what was the term that Lebedev used? Tra...no. Troaning. Yes, that's it, Troaning! According to legend, the center of the crystallite would glow with healing properties. The most important thing about his memory, the thing which excited him the most was that he had come across the translation of Troaning quite by accident. The addition of the discovery had boosted his grade up one and a half points. The English translation of Troaning just happened to be....Lord this couldn't be a coincidence, Thinning! Pastor Lockhart did three things successively, he headed towards the attic to locate his paper, he grabbed his cell phone and hit the speed dial for the Martinez's cell phone and he prayed..."Lord please have mercy on your children."

Looking around Doctor Thomas's office Anzel decided that it was sparse but comfortable. But, why so much green in her décor? Decor? Oh brother, he'd been watching too much HGTV with Katrina lately. Doctor Thomas's achievement display was pretty impressive. It looked like she had more degrees than a thermometer, but her collection of Hindu wall hangings and statues gave him a pounding headache. Seeing Katrina notice his hand wringing made Anzel work to regain some composure. He gave her a reassuring wink and blew a kiss in her direction. Pila came through the door just as Anzel's lips were puckering. Pila cleared her throat to cover a smile at the sudden flush on Anzel's cheeks. He looked so uncomfortable during the initial greetings that Pila offered him her cup of water. The cup trembled between his hands as recognition lit in his eyes. Realizing who she was transported Anzel back to those days of shame and terror. Pila silently watched Anzel's reaction with deep compassion. Seeing the softness in the doctor's eyes helped Anzel to dial back his emotions a couple of notches. Pila excused herself for a few minutes to give him time to collect himself. When she returned five minutes later, Anzel was feigning relaxation, which was common in her newer patients. "Well Mr. Martinez, it's good to see you again after so many years." Looking a little shaken, Anzel cleared his throat. Before he could respond, Katrina jumped to her feet causing him to start nervously. She stood and leaned over and touched Anzel's face, looking deeply into his eyes. He gave her his, "OOH my sweet chicka," look, causing her to giggle like a young girl. Grateful for this glimpse of her old Anzel, she threw a shy peek at Pila and let herself out of the office. "Okay Mr. Mart..." Pila began. "Call me Anzel, please." He felt a little more relaxed with Katrina out of the room. Carefully wording her approach, she began again, "Anzel, you were one of the main children who concerned me during Rasta Jones' reign of terror. I had often wondered what happened to you." Feeling a knot suddenly form in his throat, Anzel asked timidly, "Do you know what happened to Wesley?" Rushing ahead he added, "I used to have nightmares about Linwood. I would dream that I would be trying to rescue Wesley, always trying to keep him from falling or drowning. I would just barely grab a hold of his hand and I could see the stark terror in his eyes.

He would plead with me, "save me Anzel!" Then he would slip from my grasp. It always ended the same way. His last words were always, "It's your fault he got me Anzel." Not hearing any response from Doctor Thomas, Anzel looked up and caught her troubled expression. Sighing she said, "Anzel, I can only share this classified information with you now because the case has been closed for over a decade. Also because there are no surviving members of Wesley's immediate family. I'm telling you this because I feel like I owe you that much." She continued with difficulty, "Approximately eleven years after that cover up at Linwood concerning you boys." Pila paused at Anzel's sharp intake of breath at the words cover up. "Yes, Linwood was good for sweeping things neatly under the rug. Yes, as tragic as that situation was, the director wanted to make sure that his reputation went untarnished. Sadly, Wesley and his family died in a mysterious house fire. Although the neighbors reported a suspicious looking young man with red dreadlocks in the area right before the fire, arson was ruled out as the cause of the blaze." Anzel quickly leaned forward in his seat, startling Pila. "Why didn't anyone from Linwood come forward and give the police Rasta's history? Doctor Thomas, why didn't you? You knew him, you knew what a monster he really was." The look of raw pain that crossed Pila's face, made Anzel ashamed that he blew up at her. Speaking softly, she defended herself with, "Well Anzel, my hands were tied by patient, doctor confidentiality. How could I have proven the truth? I had no evidence for the police to go on, only my suspicions. Finally, after all these years I can admit, I feared Rasta's violent behavior, and I still fear it today."

Highly distressed, Anzel roughly pulled his hands through

his hair and spoke quietly, "Oh, sure...of course." Looking at the thick mane of Anzel's hair spill over his shoulders made Pila absentmindedly twist the strands of her post meno-pausal bob. She forced her mind back to the matters at hand. "Soothingly, Pila said, "Alright Anzel, why don't you start at the beginning. When did your first dream occur? Please speak slowly so that I can have an accurate account." One hour later which included a lot of stopping and prompting from Pila a perspiration drenched Anzel gave Pila an amazing piece of the puzzle. He claimed that not only did he believe that Rasta was summoning him, but that his God was also urging him to go and minister to this demon possessed man. Visit a man who has been haunting his dreams for almost twenty years. Startled at Anzel's reference to demonic possession, Pila sat forward and knocked over her cup of lukewarm herbal tea. She dis-tractedly dabbed at the spill with a hand full of tissues that promised softness as well as strength. Deep in thought, she all but forgot about her patient, and nearly jumped out of her skin when Anzel cleared his throat. Slightly irritated, she tried to continue in a professional manner. Well Anzel, if I hadn't ex-perienced Rasta Jones for myself, with personal contact to go along with my detailed records, which I do have in safe keep-ing, I would probably recommend my own personal therapist to you. She really is very good." Anzel spoke up quickly, "That wouldn't have been necessary Doctor Thomas, my God who I mentioned earlier, is a mind regulator and a heart fixer. Even though I don't fully understand things right now, I know that the plans he has for me are for good and not evil...." Tight lipped, Pila interrupted, "Please, let's keep this on an entirely medical level." Let's leave your religious beliefs out of this."

Feeling the tension in the air, Pila knew she lost Anzel's trust. Slightly flushed, he responded firmly, "With all due respect to your professional title Doctor Thomas, if my belief is anything, it is not religious. It is a valuable, personal relationship with Jesus Christ. Everything in my life is leading me to the day that I will be with Him in eternity. Eternity is a long time Doctor Thomas, don't you think?" Before Pila could respond there was a light tap at the door. Katrina stuck her head inside and her expectant smile froze on her lips in the chilly atmosphere. Rising quickly, Anzel gave a curt nod in Pila's general direction and grabbed Katrina's arm and whisked her out of the room. "Anzel, wha...?" His scathing look severed her question in half...Looking down, Katrina whispered, "What now Lord?"

The ride home was frigidly quiet. Anzel threw resentful looks at Katrina with every opportunity allowed while he drove. Katrina busied herself by checking the messages on Anzel's cell phone. Three bill collectors, one from Cleet Brown, "Hey buddy, we miss you, is everything okay?" She repeated the message to Anzel and was rewarded with a sour look. The last message was from Pastor Lockhart. Katrina sat up suddenly and almost caused Anzel to slam on the brakes. "Hey what's gotten into you?" Katrina threw up her hand to shush him and he scowled in response. Anzel knew that this situation was putting a lot of stress on his family, but he and Katrina were never this rude and disrespectful to each other. This had to stop now. "Baby I'm Sor...." he began, but stopped short at the excited look on Katrina's face. Pushing the disconnect button Katrina gave Anzel a great big smile, fully dimple loaded. Not being able to help smiling back at her, he waited for her explanation. Looking very mysterious, she said, "You get me to me Casa, Sue Casa in one piece and I will give you some good news." Knowing Katrina would not budge, Anzel shrugged and asked instead, "Is your mom bringing my babies home today? I need to see my Muchachas"...Katrina looked at her familiar, relaxed husband, nodded yes, and decided to enjoy the rest of the ride home.

Chapter 9

Footsteps to Miles'

When they arrived home, Katrina, under the threat of intense tickling, revealed her secret. The message from their equally excited pastor was that he had what he felt was a major piece of the mystery and would like to come over as soon as possible. They returned his call as soon as they had settled in and touched base with the girls. Twenty minutes later Dijin hid his grin as he noticed Anzel quickly ducking out of the window when he pulled onto the opposite side of the street. Opening the door, Anzel coughed to cover an involuntary chuckle himself as he watched his pastor unfold his large frame from his wife's tiny Volkswagen. The pastor glanced around as he smoothed out his rumpled flannel shirt and faded dungarees. He gave a slightly embarrassed nod to Anzel and cleared his throat. Salvaging as much dignity as he could he crossed the street and quickly approached Anzel and shook his hand. Knowing that Anzel was trying to hide his amusement, Dijin decided to have some fun with him. "Well you could have at least given this old codger a hand instead of standing there laughing." He looked so serious that Anzel immediately turned red. "And while you're spending so much of your renewed energy cackling at your favorite pastor, go there to the trunk of my car and get that dusty old briefcase." Not able to hold onto the scowl, Dijin burst out laughing. "Look at your face Anzel. Man, you are way too serious. I was just teasing you hombre. But I really do need that brief case though." "Oh, sure, sure." Anzel said, scurrying away, looking like He didn't get the joke. Puzzled, Dijin scratched his head. Maybe Ella was right, maybe he was the only one who thought his jokes were hilarious. Oh well, he was a riot at the senior center on Tuesdays. They thought he was a hoot. Ella was sure they meant coot though. Of course a large percentage of them wore hearing aids. Smirking at himself, he went in search of Katrina's famous sweet potato tarts...ah, one of the simple pleasures of his life.

Twenty minutes later, Anzel, Katrina and Dijin were surrounded by yellowed, type written pages, empty coffee cups and Styrofoam plates holding the barest of tart crumbs. Anzel was pouring over the paragraphs that Dijin had highlighted. Dijin rubbed his stomach contentedly, "Katrina, your sweet potato tarts have to come straight from heaven." Flashing Pastor Lockhart one of her special dimples, she said shyly, "Thanks pastor, have another one." Looking tempted to say yes, Dijin regretfully looked at the buttons straining over his ample belly, and said, "Thanks, but I'll pass." Anzel was totally fascinated and absorbed with the Uriankhai Monks and the forbidden practice of Troaning. Finishing the last highlighted paragraph, he sat back on the couch and sighed mournfully. "Imagine, having that kind of dedication and focus. Imagine sacrificing your whole life as a means of possessing something." Then, looking at Dijin with a troubled expression, he asked, "What does any of this have to do with my dilemma?" Pastor Lockhart responded quickly, "That's what we are asking God to reveal to us son." "Pastor?" Katrina interrupted, "You mentioned that Troaning and Thinning have very similar meanings?" Dijin nodded yes in Katrina's direction without taking his eyes off of Anzel. The object of his intense scrutiny was becoming more and more agitated. Suddenly Anzel jumped up, excused himself over the startled protests of Dijin and Katrina. He grabbed his jacket and left through the side door, leading to the garage. Moments later, a resigned pastor and tearful, confused wife, listened to sounds of Anzel's car starting and backing up. The shrill sound of a horn caused Katrina and Dijin to jump. "Lord, please don't let Anzel have an accident," said a concerned Katrina... Dijin tried to comfort Katrina, assuring her that he and Ella would be earnestly praying.

Approximately eight hours later, after Katrina and the twins had been in bed for quite some time, she listened to Anzel fumbling with his key in the door. She sighed wearily wondering what drama this night would bring. Feeling stretched beyond her limits of understanding her beloved Anzel, Katrina softly quoted one of her mother's favorite bible verses. *"Come unto Me all ye that labor and are heavy laden, and I will give you rest."* Listening to the shower running from the master bathroom, she made a tough decision that she would not mention one word to Anzel about his rudeness to their pastor, or her hours of worry and fear. Exhaustion tugged at Katrina's eyes and she was lulled away by the sound of the water. Anzel's damp hair spilling over her right shoulder woke her up. Anzel mumbled a warm apology into her neck. Turning to study his finely chiseled face and dark, smoky eyes, she broke her promise and took a breath to ask him why, but Anzel quickly covered her lips with a long kiss that took her breath away. Abruptly ending the kiss, he held up a warning hand and said, "My name is Ricky Plain." Their serious signal. Katrina clamped her lips closed and turned away, Stung...as Anzel hoarsely whispered, "I promise to tell you everything in the morning, me chicka. Just trust God and trust me too, okay?" Katrina gave a stiff nod, a loud sniffle and a long sigh...then she turned and crawled into Anzel's waiting arms.

Breakfast the next morning consisted of the twin's favorite thing in the whole world. They loved Belgian waffle day with daddy. They also loved them covered with powdered sugar, which Anzel always put on the end of his nose to make them scream with giggles. He would purposely pretend that he didn't know, and they fell for it every time. Katrina wanted to join in the easy laughter and banter but her emotions were too much on edge. She just leaned against the storage bin and studied her family. Anzel was so handsome, with his olive complexion and dark hair and eyes. Both girls looked just like their dad. Both had long dark silky hair and beautiful dark brown eyes that snapped almost to black with intense emotions. Ruefully, she ran her hands through her newly colored hairdo, thinking about the way that Anzel always raved about what he called her luscious chocolate skin and her almond shaped hazel eyes. One of the things she really loved about her husband was his passionate use of words. "Okay Martinez's, break it up now. It's time for the school bus to collect two little girls." "Oh Mom!" They groaned in unison. Looking sheepish Anzel said, "You hear your mother, we will continue this on the next waffle day." More giggles, which faded as the girls raced out the front door at the sound of their bus pulling up. Finally, with the girls gone and the breakfast dishes dried and put away, Katrina turned and faced an amused Anzel. Crossing her arms, she waited unsmiling for him to speak. Anzel came around the kitchen table and took Katrina by the hands and led her into the living room. He gestured towards their favorite recliner, and sitting down, he guided her to his knees. Wrapping his arms tightly around her, he held her for a few minutes just listening to her breathe. Katrina, sensing the Lord telling her to be still, swallowed the questions crowding her throat. It took several seconds before she realized that Anzel had started talking, because his voice was so low. Now she had to catch up with what he was saying. "And when I saw that Pastor Dijin really didn't have a solid answer, it was like I just lost it. I just had to get away from everything." At Katrina's sharp intake of breath, Anzel stopped talking and squeezed her tighter in his embrace. "No! Not you and the girls, chicka, you know I would never mean that." Tears of relief spilled over onto Katrina's cheeks. Anzel turned her around and traced her face and momentarily lost his train of thought. "Hey sweetie, what did you do to your hair?" He quickly added, "I love it." Then, "Katrina, do you believe me when I say that no one and nothing apart from God Himself, could ever take me away from you and our girls? Do you? I would die for you Katrina, you have to know that. Surely you know that you are the only one for me in this life." Katrina nodded slowly. "Where were you for half of the night?" Tensely he answered, "I went back Katrina. I had to see for myself that it wasn't just a terrible figment of my imagination. As awful as it was, I had to know that it was real." Releasing her held breath, Katrina asked, "Was it Anzel, was it real?" "It was very real chicka. There Linwood stood like some dark ancient beast, rising up out of the earth to strangle my life away. I stood there, shivering, holding onto that cold metal fence and remembering that crazy fear. Fear that helped shape and mold me into who I am today. Katrina, you don't know what fear is like to a man. You have this image, you know, this male machismo. You have to be this tough macho, cardboard person, and all the while there's this fear like lead in your belly, threatening to escape at the first sign of weakness. It's loco girl. I couldn't even admit to God that I was scared, so I buried it deep inside. I remember, I tried to talk to my dad about it one time. I don't know what I expected from him, but I was a kid you know? I was just a boy who had been through this unbelievable trauma. He said, "Forget it. A man gets over things." "I wasn't a man, I was a boy." Anzel shook his head bitterly. "After that it was like he couldn't even look me in the eye. So I became a man and got over it, and buried it so deep, that it was forgotten, almost. But God knew it was like a cancer, eating away at me, keeping me from being whole. Why else would He let that monster come back into my life? Why Katrina? Why would God allow that?" Wrapping her arms around Anzel, she murmured against the soft hair she loved so much. "God will show us babe. I know He will."...But she was thinking, "Will you show us Lord? Will you put an end to this torture?

Chapter 10

'Living Among Ashes'

At four o'clock in the morning, Anzel was in the clutches of the most terrifying episode of his nightmare series yet. The dream began in the usual way. It was the same inevitable journey that would lead Anzel to the mirror in the apartment. Only this time when Anzel's hands reached for the horns protruding from his own head, the figure in the mirror reached out and grabbed Anzel's wrists. Kicking and yelling, he was pulled into the mirror. Pinning both of his arms cruelly to his sides, Rasta held him in a crushing embrace. Anzel struggled to breathe, feeling the darkness trying to swallow him. Rasta's putrid breath bathed his face as he screamed in malicious glee. With his last ounce of strength, Anzel whispered, "Jesus, help me!" Rasta's eyes bugged in horrified surprise. Screaming, he let go of Anzel and covered his ears. Released from the hellish grip, Anzel fell backwards out of the mirror. Instead of landing on the floor of the apartment as he expected, he landed on the floor of his and Katrina's bedroom. Sprawled there with his heart racing and sweat pouring down his face, he gave thanks to God. Dazed he looked around the bedroom until he spotted Katrina's sleeping form. He gave a huge sigh of relief. He was really in that apartment this time. Really in the mirror with that monster, Rasta. A sharp pain shot through the old bite mark on his arm as if to bear witness of this fact. Touching the permanent teeth marks, white hot rage filled him. Just as quickly it dissolved as despair took over. Carefully rising on wobbly legs, he made his way to the patio…to have a desperate talk with The Lord.

At the exact same hour, several miles away in her gated community, Doctor Pila Thomas tossed restlessly, in the throes of her own nightmare. Still asleep, she swiped angrily at the tears running down, and across her face, christening her pillow. She was ten years old again, back on the rubber plantation of her childhood. She and her sister Ryia were giggling and chasing each other in and out of the trees. As they came near an irrigation ditch, Pila stopped and stared at it. Ryia, realizing that Pila was no longer chasing her, came back and stood directly in front of the ditch, blocking Pila's view. Knowing what was coming next, she opened her mouth to warn her sister, but before she could utter one word, Rasta Jones stepped out from behind a nearby rubber tree with a hideous grin on his face. Pila stood speechless, frozen by terror, as Rasta grabbed the seemingly unaware Ryia, and in one swift motion, he pulled out a large blade and made a deep slash across her throat. Pila felt the merciful fingers of oblivion yanking her away from the grisly sight. Just before her mind shut down, she watched as Rasta dipped his grinning mouth to Ryia's throat and begin to drink her blood…Blackness covered Pila as she fainted dead away in her sleep.

At the same moments that Anzel was being pulled into the mirror and Rasta was stepping out from behind the rubber tree, Dijin was propelled awake by an urgency to pray for Anzel and someone who was a stranger to him. "And Katrina too Lord?" His heart received a quick "yes." When Pastor Dijin Lockhart felt the Clarion call to prayer, he didn't hesitate...he quickly fell to his knees and answered the call like the warrior that he was.

Because Katrina's back was to Anzel when he tumbled onto the bedroom floor, he didn't see her sleeping, tearstained face. She is having a nightmare of her own. She is walking in a strange, yet familiar place. Her feet feel heavy, as if they are submerged in something thick. Her eyes dart back and forth fearfully. She is terrified for Anzel. Why? She doesn't know. A few yards ahead, she spots a dilapidated building. Peering through the open doorway, she sees Anzel. Flooded with relief she calls out, "Anzel!", but her voice makes no sound. The door slams shut, sending her into a panic. She tries to force her feet to move faster, but even as she bursts through the cracked and peeling door, she is trapped in that dream quality motion. Catching a glimpse of Anzel, she sees him disappear through an apartment door at the end of the hallway. Something is so familiar about all of this but she can't put her finger on it. It is hard to reason, because her mind is sluggish with fear. The door through which Anzel has disappeared has two glowing numbers on it, a six and a zero. Something teases her memory, but is ripped away when she hears Anzel's hoarse scream. "Anzel! I'm coming, Anzel!" She yells soundlessly. Reaching the door, she throws it open not knowing what to expect. She is amazed as she stands staring at an almost empty apartment. She looks curiously at the large gilded mirror propped against the wall. Where could Anzel have gone? Katrina slowly approaches the mirror. "NO!" Helplessly she tries to obey the warning, but she knows that she has to play this dream scene out unto the end. The mirror briefly holds onto the image of a slender, pretty African American woman, before transforming into a wolverine with red, dreaded hair, bloody dripping fangs and horns protruding from the sides of his head. Before the scream in her belly can reach her paralyzed throat, the apparition in the mirror smiles at her with bloody teeth and in a childlike voice says, "I don't like you, you give me a pain, and for your information my name is....Ricky Plain." Katrina screams and begins to stumble backwards, when the beast reaches out and grabs her arms in a vicious grip and pulls her towards the mirror. She feels herself being swallowed up in darkness. Her frozen limbs are unresponsive to her pleading. At the instant that the mirrored monster is about to possess her completely, the desperate plea, "Jesus!" Bursts from her lips. The face of Pastor Lockhart appears over the wolf man's shoulder. Sensing something behind himself, he releases Katrina. Just before crashing onto her bed, she hears Dijins fading prayer..." Lord please cover Katrina Martinez in the precious blood of the Lamb. Keep her safe from all evil, in Jesus name I pray, Amen."

Katrina's eyes shot open. Wildly she searched the room for Anzel. Gone. She filled her starving lungs with air as she tried to calm her heart and think. What just happened? Did she leave this room? "Oh my God." she whimpered. "I've got to find Anzel." Looking at the digital clock she took note of the time. It was a few minutes after four am. "The patio, that's where Anzel would be at this hour." She threw the covers off and stood too quickly, which her spinning head revealed to her. She fought off waves of dizziness and nausea. Sharply she commanded her feeble legs to carry her to her husband. Katrina didn't know why she felt this urgency to get to Anzel, but something was telling her to hurry. Lurching in the direction of the bedroom door, she felt an overwhelming sense of foreboding as she found herself saying, "I'm coming Anzel." Detouring, she hurriedly stuck her head into the twin's bedroom, satisfied of their safety, she ran on towards the patio on much stronger legs. "Anzel!" She spotted him through the patio doors. Fascination at his actions stopped Katrina dead in her tracks. What was he doing? Who was he talking to? Was he crying? He's crying? Puzzled, she watched as he angrily swiped a tear away. Automatically she lifted her hand towards the door, wanting to bring comfort, to hold him and kiss away his tears, but…what is…this? Anzel raised his head and looked directly into Katrina's eyes. Seeing her raised hand, he lifted his own towards her as a strange look came over his face. Then poof! He vanished right before her eyes! "Mommy, mommy?" Groggily Katrina peered up at her daughter's faces, vaguely wondering why she was lying on the inside patio floor. Then her memory hit her. Anzel! The impossible memory of what she saw propelled her to her feet and she startled the twins. They began to cry in unison as she ran onto the patio. "Oh my God!" She screamed. "It wasn't a dream. It was real. Anzel, where are you? Where did you go sweetie?" The girls became hysterical, pulling at Katrina's clothes and crying for their daddy. Dazed, Katrina slid to the ground, holding the pile of night clothes that had been covering her husband before he disappeared into thin air…she couldn't take her eyes off of the spatters of dried blood.

The crime scene investigators had come and gone and

Katrina's parents had rushed in and rescued the girls. Anzel's family had been notified and now the only ones left in the Martinez home was Katrina, the Lockhart's and a very suspicious Federal Investigator. Agent Justine Polk, head of the Special Missions Unit Concerning Kidnapping, a.k.a., S.M.U.C.K. Agent Polk was of medium build with intense violet colored eyes. She wore her dark hair in a severe, no nonsense bun with an unforgiving part down the center. She squirmed with impatience as Katrina Martinez tried to put her trauma into intelligible words. Clearly this wasn't an assignment for her division. This was probably a case for the psych ward. Or was it? Because there was blood on the missing husband's pajama shirt, and what also looked like bruising around the suspect's wrist. The lab was running the results now and she was waiting for a text. Her lab buddy owed her a favor, so she was getting rush results. If there was anything suspicious about Katrina Martinez, she would pick it up. They called her 'the nose', behind her back on the force, but she was secretly proud of the name. It earned her respect among her predominant peers. The more that Katrina tried to explain the thing that her eyes tried to convince her was true, the more panicked she became. Wildly her eyes grabbed at Dijin. He patted her hand and gestured at Ella to come over to them. "Agent Polk, If you will allow me, I'll explain to you what Mrs. Martinez was able to relay to my wife and myself earlier." Looking at Katrina's stricken face, Agent Polk directed her next question in a softer tone. "Mrs. Martinez, will you confirm that the information given on your behalf by Mr. Dijin Lockhart will be true and consistent with the statements in your police report, to the best of your ability?" Katrina nodded her head, with dazed eyes. "Okay Mr. Lockhart, you may begin, Oh excuse me please?" Agent Polk unclipped her cell phone to answer her text chirp. She glanced up at Katrina with a puzzled expression on her face. "Mrs. Martinez, were you and your husband and children alone in the house last night?" "Yes, yes of course." Katrina mumbled. Agent Polk studied Katrina for a long moment as if wondering if she should continue. Going ahead she said, "Oddly, the blood sample that was on the front of your husband's shirt, was not yours or your husband's. Frankly, I find the results startling. The blood belongs to a career criminal. He is a vicious, man who is a permanent resident of a maximum security facility, of which I'm not allowed to disclose the location of." Katrina, Dijin and Ella, sat with unreleased breath as she spoke. " Okay I need you three to sign this release of responsibility form before we go any further, and I'm going to have to have my partner Agent Harris to step in and witness all three signatures." When the procedure was completed, the agent gave Katrina, Dijin and Ella, each a lengthy stare before asking, "Do any of you know a man named Rasta Jones?" Agent Polk, who had witnessed every facet of human nature, was completely taken aback at the reaction to the name Rasta Jones. Mrs. Martinez, burst out crying, while Mr. and Mrs. Lockhart's faces drained of blood. "Alright someone had better do some explaining." Agent Polk said all business now. Dijin looked at Katrina, "May I?" She nodded weakly. "Agent Polk", Dijin began. "You must realize that we are dealing with some things completely beyond the norm." She gave a grudging nod. "What I need to do is fill you in on everything that's happened so far and that will bring you up to the events of this morning." "Go on", the agent urged. "You're going to find this impossible to believe but bear with me. We do know Rasta Jones, although none of us in this room has ever personally met him." As Dijin shared the story of Anzel and Rasta, Agent Polk fought to retain her impassive expression. Finishing, the recounting of Anzel's plight left Dijin newly grieved. "Leading up to this morning, we, my wife and I received a frantic phone call around seven o'clock. You would probably call it a coincidence, because Katrina happens to be one of the three people I had been praying for several hours earlier. I'd like to refer to it as divine providence from The Most High God." The emotion Dijin felt was evident in his voice. "Sir please just stick to the facts." Agent Polk said, with a determined deadpan face. Blushing slightly, Dijin said, "Oh sorry, let's see, at first the sounds on the phone were incoherent, and I had to search for my glasses to read the caller ID. After discovering that it was Katrina, uh sorry, Mrs. Martinez, we decided it would be better to just come to her home." "Really?" The agent asked suspiciously. Are you in the habit of visiting people's homes early in the morning?" Flustered, Dijin responded with, "I am a pastor Agent Polk. I will do whatever is necessary to comfort the flock that God has given me charge over. I know this seems like foolishness to you, but in the body of Christ, we are expected to show God's love and care and often mercy for each other. If it means that I look foolish, then so be it. If It means that my motives will be misunderstood sometimes, then God Himself will intervene on my behalf. May I continue?" The agent's face held a grudging respect and she said softly, "Please go on sir." "It took us approximately twenty minutes to arrive. We discovered Mrs. Martinez and her two daughters in a state of hysteria. My wife took control of the girls, Asharia and

Kiamara, while I worked to calm their mother down. After my wife was able to get the girls comfortable with breakfast and a video, Katrina allowed Ella to serve her some hot tea. She calmed down enough to tell us this…" Looking at Agent Polk carefully Dijin continued. "She told us that she had awakened from a pretty horrific nightmare, to find that Mr. Martinez was absent from their bedroom. She went looking for her husband to ease her anxiety from the dream. She spotted him on the patio, where he had lately been spending the wee hours of the morning," At that statement the agent shot Dijon a sharp look. "Mrs. Martinez said that she watched him for a few minutes because she could hear him talking to someone. Then looking through the patio doors she could see that he was alone. She said that he looked very agitated, and that it appeared that he was crying. Then she said…she said that…, well what she said was….she saw her husband of ten years, the love of her life, the father of her two children…her best friend in the… whole world, disappear, vanish, like poof! Into thin air." After a lengthy silence, Pastor Lockhart looked Agent Polk squarely in the eye and said, "As The Lord God Jehovah is my righteous judge and witness, and as incredible as this sounds, as difficult as this will be to explain to your superiors. I would swear in a court of law that I have never, ever known this God fearing young woman to tell anything except the absolute truth… Whatever you or the law officials decide, we are telling the unadulterated truth.

Pila hung up the phone with a bewildered grimace. She thought she had seen the last of the Martinez's. Running her hand through her unkempt bob, her ring caught painfully on a tender patch of hair. "Ouch!" Pulling her ring free, rewarded

her with a small cluster of hair wrapped around her extrava-
gant diamond wedding ring. It was one of her few spoils from
the battlefield that was her former marriage. Why she still
wore it on her opposite hand was still untapped ground to
Pila and her therapist. Fifteen years later her ex husband was
still causing her to lose her hair. She smiled ruefully at the
state of mind she was in these days. She forced her mind back
to the matter at hand. Boy she needed to get her own life.
She had agreed to meet with Katrina Martinez after hearing
the incredible details surrounding the disappearance of Anzel.
Wistfully glancing at the twelve inch statue of a Hindu deity
on her clock table, she spoke to it as she did each morning.
"What have I gotten myself into this time?" As was the norm
each morning, the statue's response was slack eyed silence.
For some reason this morning the silence reminded Pila of
just how alone she was, in this world…Then as if to express
an agreement, the patch of scalp surrounding her ripped out
strands of hair, began to sting and throb in earnest.

Chapter 11

'Falling Into Grace'

A nzel Martinez was falling; he was falling head over feet into a swirling gray void. He had been falling for an endless amount of time now. He didn't know how long, and several times he had lost consciousness, only to be revived by a bitter cold, soundless wind. The constant falling motion caused his stomach to threaten to erupt. Anzel gritted his teeth against the raw nauseating fear in his gut. Desperately, he tried to remember a prayer, any words that would take away this mind numbing terror. Slowly he felt his grip on reality slipping away. The secure presence he'd always felt from God was fading. He found this more frightening than anything else. Mouth frozen open in an silent yawn of fear, he fell deeper into the throat of the…dragon? Lord help him, that's what it felt like. The constant free fall was taking a toll on Anzel's body as well as his sanity. Violent tremors caused his limbs to splay out at odd, impossible angles while he looked on helplessly. Was this some new hideous nightmare? If so, he doubted if his heart could take the stress. It was sure to kill him. Maybe he was already dead. Anzel searched his mind for something, anything to cling to. His beloved Katrina's face appeared behind his tightly closed eyelids. Sluggishly, his mind fought to collect his bearings. He could visualize Katrina's look of shock before the ground opened up and swallowed him. How was that possible? Had an earthquake occurred? Anzel's analytical mind tried to kick in. Shouldn't he have hit the bottom by now, if he had actually fallen in a hole in the earth? The insane free falling was not slowing, but the fear and nausea he was feeling earlier was disappearing. Memories began filling his mind. He had been walking around the patio, trying to shake off the latest terrible dream, talking to The Lord to ward off a panic attack. He remembered that he had gotten angry and had begun to yell at the sky. Then movement inside the house caused him to look up and he saw Katrina's eyes wide with sorrow and her hand reaching towards him. Lifting his own hand in response, he froze as the shadowy image of Rasta Jones, superimposed itself over Katrina. Then, he was gone, falling. An inhuman wail coming from somewhere below, forced his mind back to his present situation. Chilled to the bone, Anzel could only jerk with spasms, shiver and plead with God for rescue as he continued to fall into the abyss. A question formed in his mind, drowning out his frantic prayers, "What was waiting for him at the bottom of this dark hole?" He knew, just as much as he knew anything, that whatever it was...it was waiting for him.

A nervous police officer on duty outside of a room in the Intensive Care Unit of Bellview Community Hospital shuddered at the guttural moans coming from the newly admitted inmate, Rasta Jones. Even though the patient was unconscious and handcuffed to the metal bed frame, and even though there was a heavy glass door between them, the veteran officer was still very uneasy. Backup was less than thirty seconds away, fully armed. Squaring his shoulders and applying his poker face, he watched as two attractive, reluctant nurses approached to take the inmate's vital signs. They looked as if they'd rather be petting piranha fish during feeding time. He gave them a tight smile and a commiserating nod and followed them into the room. It was always a shock at the first glance of the apparition in the hospital bed. His thin feral features, along with the filthy cascade of red dreadlocks did not look human. The most unsettling thing, about him was the sharp, yellowed teeth protruding from both corners of his cracked, bleeding lips. Even motionless, with both wrists shackled to the bed, Rasta Jones looked ready to attack at a moment's notice. The rumors surrounding his suicide attempt were causing quite a stir at Bellview. The bizarre circumstances would be fodder for the next urban legend. Rumor to non prison employees…but fact to those who were unfortunate enough to be inside the walls with Rasta Jones.

These were the facts surrounding Rasta Jones' attempt on his life….Co Chaplain Cleet brown's evening sessions with his scheduled inmates, began normal enough. He was feeling a little guilty because he had been ignoring Rasta's requests to speak with him. Also he was still in shock about the disappearance of Anzel Martinez. Shaking off the feeling of unease, he waited to be accompanied by two officers who were there to insure his safety. As they entered the pen containing Rasta's cell a heavy cloak of dread slid around Cleet's shoulders. The other inmates were unnaturally quiet in their cells as the two wary looking officers led the way. Cleet felt a powerful urge in his spirit to begin pleading the blood over himself and covering the two officers. Something felt terribly wrong. He noticed the hesitation in both officers' footsteps as they closed in on the cell. Cleet glanced around the block at the faces pressed against the cell bars. Expressions ranged from flat, blank stares to fear, but no one was talking. The signal was given to the main control panel operator and Rasta's cell door began to slide open. Before they could tell the prisoner to stand down, the grisly scene stole their breath. Unable to stop his momentum, Cleet's feet carried him into the worst bloodbath he had ever seen. Backing themselves and Cleet out of the cell, one officer was already radioing for help. Cleet felt his lunch of Buffalo Chicken wings and blue cheese dressing rising like a volcano. Searching wildly for an escape, too late, he erupted! The jagged slash across Rasta's throat would haunt his dreams for months to come. Even more disturbing than the amount of infectious blood in that cell, and more chilling than that self inflicted slash, was that grin, that frightening ear to ear grin and the vacant stare. Cleet shuddered as a chill raced up his spine. Much later, sitting at his parent's kitchen table, over thirty miles away from the prison, he had an iron grip on his fourth cup of black coffee. The cups of coffee along with the handmade quilt his mother had wrapped around his shoulders, still didn't quell his shakes. The litany of a childhood song kept riding over and over through his mind. "Who's afraid of the boogey man, the boogey man, the boogey man, who's afraid of the boogey man, he'll get you while you sleep, he'll get you while you wake....he will get you"...to be sure Rasta Jones was the closest thing to a real life boogey man that Cleet had ever seen.

Anzel must have blacked out again, because his eyes shot open in response to his thigh muscles cramping. Groaning, he tried to straighten against the pull of gravity. On and on he dropped, helplessly being swallowed by the black hole.

The eerie animal noises coming from below vibrated in his ears. "God where am I? Katrina? God please help me!" Anzel's mouth moved but no sound came out. Just when he was about to spiral into despair, a feeling of peace infused his entire being. A familiar assurance enveloped him. It was God. It had to be, but here, in this place? The presence of God slowly wound around him, securing him in a protective cocoon. Feeling the strain ease from his legs, he realized that he was in a sitting position now. It was almost as though he fit into the palm of someone's hand. A voice poured over Anzel's troubled soul like a soothing stream. His being yearned towards the words of his Savior. "Anzel? Anzel? Do you want to see what real love looks like? Would you like to share my heart's desire? Listen to me, my son. I Am, is sending you on a fishing expedition. I am trusting you to bring back something very precious to me. I have paid a great price for this treasure. It is a very difficult thing that I am asking of you. Fear not, I have set you like flint I have qualified you, after I have chosen you. I require a tremendous sacrifice from you, but I have designed you for this purpose, for this connection. Endure as a good soldier, keep the faith, and be strong. Remember My words, *"Greater love has no man than this, that he will lay down his life for a friend."* It is The Thinning! Pray that your faith will not fail you. Keep my words close to your heart in times of battle. Lo I will be with you always, even until the end of the world. Also consider this, it is the Love Agape' that will overcome the wicked one. Love and truth. Be strong Anzel, in the power of My might and you will receive the promise." Anzel's heart rate began to speed up. Panicking, it became very hard for him to breathe. More heavenly reassurance filled his heart and slowed its pace.

"I have given you a new heart, a soldier's heart. You now have a supernatural love that will overcome the evil in this place." Anzel felt his heart straining against his rib cage...There was a white hot pain, then blessed nothingness.

Chapter 12

'Twice Shy'

D octor Pila Thomas sat staring at the cold curry and rice congealing on her expensive china. She wrestled with a request she'd received, a request that robbed her completely of her appetite. Doctor Maylon Tessker, head of the Neurology Department at Bellview Community Hospital, had called, soliciting her help in a serious matter concerning a patient who happened to be an inmate. Coincidence? When he mentioned Rasta's name, Pila's stomach clenched painfully and threatened to expel it's curry and rice contents. Rasta Jones. "Whoa, Pila just hear him out," she cautioned herself." Pila was horrified with herself that she was a tiny bit relieved at Rasta's tragic condition, it shamed her. That guilt over her unprofessional attitude influenced her to agree to meet Doctor Tessker in forty eight hours at Rasta's bedside. Sharing her expertise about a case used to be a feather in Pila's cap, but expertise or none, she didn't want to come within spitting distance of this... monster...patient. Quickly, she speed dialed her therapist. Forty eight hours later and battling conflicting emotions, Pila gawked at the wasted shell lying in the hospital bed. Rasta was hooked up to machines that were designed to prolong life no matter how pathetic the life. Why the handcuffs? She felt more curiosity than pity. Doctor Tessker studied Pila's reaction to Rasta carefully. Mentally shaking herself, Pila made a decision to share only a small portion of what she knew about Rasta with

Doctor Tessker. Clearing her throat and looking away from the bed she asked, "Is it really necessary to keep him handcuffed to the bed? He doesn't look as if he has the strength to even sit up." She grimaced as her eyes fell on his heavily bandaged throat. Doctor Tessker kept his tone even as he replied quietly, "I'm afraid none of the staff will come near him otherwise. The reason that I found it necessary to bring in someone with your expertise in this area, is because, even though Mr. Jones is still comatose, it's obvious that he is experiencing something very traumatic. Frankly we are concerned that his heart will give out from the tremendous strain being placed upon it. Studying Pila he carefully asked, "Doctor Thomas, are you a praying woman?" Startled, Pila looked into Doctor Tessker's eyes. "No, not at all, why do you ask?" Clearing his throat and looking quickly over his shoulder, Pila noticed that a light had gone out of his eyes when he turned back to her. His next words sounded strangely monotone to Pila's trained ear. She found herself snipping off a little prick of disappointment. "I just don't know what we're dealing with here. In my thirty plus years in this field of medicine I have never encountered anyone with a history like Mr. Jones." "If you only knew what I know", Pila thought bitterly. Continuing almost in a whisper he added, "The brain scans done on this patient have waves very similar to…to, well those of a untamed animal." Pila fastened incredulous eyes on Doctor Tessker. "What are you suggesting? That we're not dealing with a human being here?" "Yes, by all appearances he is human, but…" his voice trailed off as Rasta began to hiss like a rattle snake. They both backed away from the bed in amazement as Rasta's eyes opened and looked directly at Pila…He continued to stare at the door, long after Pila had fled, followed by an incredulous Doctor Tessker and a newly resigned officer.

Chapter 13
'The Call Of The Piper'

"Katydids, you have to eat something." Katrina's mother pleaded with her sternly. Brushing the hair back from her face, she peered at her mother through sad, wistful eyes. "Mom, I'm just not hungry right now. Please leave me alone, I promise I'll eat something later." Unconvinced, she sucked her teeth, "You said that two hours ago, it's now four o'clock in the afternoon." Realizing that it would be less of a hassle to just eat something, she eyed her egg salad sandwich warily. Shakily, she came to a decision. She would put an end to this pity party and search for her dwindling faith in a loving God, Who had always seen her through every trial. New trial, same God, right? He hadn't changed in all of this. The bible says that He changes not. He is the same yesterday, today and forever. Even as her life was being torn away from her, there He sits. Unchanging. Amazing. Now, now don't let bitterness set in. She warned herself. Trying not to scowl at her sandwich, she asked her mother, "Um, where did Pop take the girls today?" The look of sadness in her mom's eye caused her brief absence from her pity party to be short lived. The tears came in a flood. Quickly her Mother gathered her in a crushing embrace. Losing herself in the familiar scent of daffodil cologne she was transported back to childhood. The sweetness pierced her heart, as the "fix every boo boo" song filled her ears. Her mother sang her unique version of "Hush little baby." But inside, her mother wept right along with her adult baby, because she herself knew that there was a price to pay for that glorious crown. That being tempered in the fire made one into a thing of beauty...in the Lord's eyes.

With his heart thundering in his ears, Rasta tried to remember how he came to be in the bottom of this dank, dark, deep pit. His pitiful cries for help ricocheted off the walls and fell back on his terrified head. Trying to stand, he found that his legs refused to obey his command. Shrill mocking laughter surrounded him and relentlessly battered him without mercy. Fragmented images of his life teased him to the edge of his sanity. Memories of his brief childhood. The tragic loss of both of his parents and the cruel treatment of his step family, compounded by the seduction of the voices in the woods. Their betrayal, which led up to his total submission to the darkness and every evil work. But the heaviest weight of all, the weight that was crushing him almost to dust, was his rejection of God's Son. Anguish twisted the scattered pieces of Rasta's soul and regret filled his entire being. Huge tears welled up in his eyes threatening to spill over, but hopelessness kept his arms pinned to his sides in defeat. He couldn't even lift a hand to wipe them away. Was he dead? He hoped so. Was this that place of torment the voices had been holding over his head for so many years, to make him do their wicked bidding? Memories of his attempt on his life came crashing into his mind. The attack in his cell, the voices pushing buttons, making his rage against himself like a driving storm. The searing pain, the pouring out of his own blood, then nothingness. He thought he was free. But now...holding his breath, he reached up and traced the jagged gash that he had ripped across his throat in rage. There had been so much of his foul, putrid blood...He giggled, tottering on the edge of complete madness, desiring to be completely mad.

Chapter 14

'The Light and the Boogeyman'

Continuing to fall, Anzel dreamed. He dreamed that he was in a large raft, flying through white water rapids. He wasn't alone in the raft, but he couldn't clearly make out the faces of the men sitting around him. Their voices were muffled but he could recognize that they were panicked. The water was foamy, icy cold and deafening. Anzel began to pray as hard as he'd ever prayed in his life. Desperately trying to see through the heavy mist, he blanched when he saw coming directly towards them a man walking across the water as calmly as if he were crossing the road. The man was wearing a long, white flowing robe. All around him the water whipped and churned, spraying him, wetting his hair and clothes. To Anzel's further amazement, the unsinkable man kept his eyes on the raft, looking neither to the left or right. The men around him cried out in fear, saying "It is a spirit." The man spoke in a voice filled with a powerful calm, "Be of good cheer, It is I, be not afraid." Then when he was a few feet away from the raft Anzel was further shocked when his own mouth opened and he spoke theses words to the stranger, "If it be thou, bid me come unto thee on the water." The man in the middle of the raging rapids said, "Come." With everything within him crying, "No!" Anzel found himself carefully working his way free from his cramped position and climbing out of the wildly bucking raft. A shock of cold water awoke him to the incredible fact that he was actually walking on the white rapids. Looking away from the stranger and staring into the churning water, he felt the push of the wind against his back and he froze in terror as he began to sink like a dead weight. He cried out, "Save me Lord!" Immediately, the stranger reached out his hands. Just before Anzel grabbed onto them he noticed deep gouges in the wrists that ran to the palms. Then he was being lifted to safety. He came awake with these words ringing in his ears, "O, thou of little faith, wherefore didst thou doubt?" Thrashing about wildly trying to get his breath, Anzel felt his hair and clothing to see if he were truly soaked. He was really there. He had felt the wind tearing at his face, tasted the foam on his lips. His hands had touched the wounds on the man's hands. "The man's hands? Jesus? I was there, I was there, I…was… there!" As the realization dawned fully on him, waves of emotion ripped through his heart. A Tsunami of awe, fear, shame and profound unworthiness. All of these emotions bled into an holy dread that threatened to consume him. The knowledge that he had touched the

hands of The Exalted Son of The Most High God, caused his ever falling body to bend into an impossibly agonizing position. Then peals of pure love infused his entire body from head to toe, forcing him to straighten in ecstasy. Anzel could only writhe and twist in unspeakable joy and agony as he continued his descent. Was this what death was like?…Oh the exquisite pleasure. Oh what joy.

Pila sat in her darkened study slowly tracing her fingertips over the same seashell pattern on the arm of her favorite wing chair. She systematically counted three hundred and thirteen traces. Backwards and forward, forward and backwards. She did this deliberately to keep control of her chaotic thoughts. It was a technique that she herself developed for her bipolar patients years ago. Am I exhibiting bipolar behavior in my old age? She smirked at her foolish thoughts, knowing that she would eventually have to face her own fears. It was always so easy to replay her famous Doctor Thomas litany to her patients, "You must face your fears head on and send them packing." Pila lifted a tremulous hand to her brow and wasn't surprised to find that she was still running a fever. She took an unappealing sip of her lukewarm latte as tiny beads of perspiration dripped onto her green silk pajamas. She blushed, in shame as her mind revisited the scene in the hospital room. She'd felt so foolish running away like that. What must Doctor Tessker think of her now? What did she care what he thought? Angrily, she shook off the last residue of attraction she'd felt towards him. She could never start a relationship with someone interested in a praying woman. Anyway, who said the man was interested? He had called and left several commiserating messages on her answering machine, but, Pila had ignored them all, along with the messages from Katrina Martinez. Her pride didn't want her to admit that she was frightened of a half dead man who was little more than a thin casing of flesh stretched over bones. This admission was humiliating to Pila who spent years building walls against violent men and useless wars and the never ending cycle of man's inhumanity to man. But the dreams. The horrible dreams. "Pila do you believe in the Rag tree man?" Ryia's seven year old voice came on the wings of a piercing memory. "The Rag tree man's gonna get you, he's gonna cut your neck and drink your blood, oh the Rag tree man's gonna get you." That hideous song from her childhood, a foolish, crazy song made up by a bunch of bored children. That's all it was, just a song. Right? With a sharp intake of breath, Pila accidentally sent her poorly balanced drink flying, spraying her pajama pant legs along with her Kermit de Frog slippers. Grabbing her throat she whimpered in a little girl's voice, Rasta is the Rag tree man…Oh Ryia, The rag tree man is real, he was always real.

In the foggy days that followed Anzel's disappearance, Katrina's state of mind coasted from blatant denial to intense desperation. When she did sleep she dreamed about Anzel. Her husband suspended in nothingness. Yet as terrible as the dreams were they gave her a strange sense of peace, which disappeared as soon as she awoke. Katrina kept trying to make sense of what her natural eyes had forever seared in her memory. Her Anzel gone. Maybe forever. This kind of agony of not knowing was almost worse than death. At least she would have some kind of closure if there were a body, something. But what did she have? A pile of empty clothing, a missing husband, and a huge…hole where her heart used to be. At least people would look at her with some understanding and compassion, and not like she had escaped from the cracker barrel. Even the few church members that showed some concern treated her carefully, as if she would blow up at the slightest provocation or break into a thousand fragmented pieces. Right now she was so alone, she was so confused…and she was so very, very angry with God.

Chapter 15

'The Hand of Mercy'

Pastor Dijin Lockhart held tightly to the hand of his frightened wife, and cried like a baby. The ambulance raced to Bellview Community Hospital. The streets were deserted at these lonely hours of the morning. Three o'clock am. Thankfully the road was clear enough for a speedy arrival. Ella's face was as white as a sheet and she could only cling to her husband's hand and mingle her tears with his. Dijin's temperature continued to soar to impossible numbers. The attendant tried to mask his concern as he worked on Dijin, by making small talk with Ella. "How long were they married?" "How many children and grandchildren did they have?" His comment about grandchildren made Ella distractedly reach up and smooth her graying curls. She tried to focus as she answered his questions in a dull monotone. Dijin's hand tightened painfully around hers as the attendant began to fit an oxygen mask over his nose and mouth. With his eyes wildly darting around, Dijin slipped away into a place of searing, white hot pain, then nothingness. The frantic activity going on in the speeding ambulance never penetrated the intense hot place in which Dijin was suspended. Misery separated Dijin from all that was previously normal to him. His body began to shake and convulse as he floated like the wisp of a shadow between life and death. Although Ella stayed as close by as they allowed her and prayed with all of the faith she possessed, Dijin was alone...As alone as he had ever been in his life.

Rasta sensed that something was coming for him, and even in this terrifying place, in which he was trapped, his fear was directed at the unknown coming to get him. Even more disturbing to him was the agitation he felt from his tormentors. Gleaning a tiny sliver of satisfaction from their confusion, allowed Rasta to weather their frenzied abuse. He cherished and held onto that satisfaction, pushing it deep inside like a hidden treasure. Rasta's curiosity overrode his fear of the unknown and in his characteristic recklessness, he screamed up into the thick darkness, "I'M RASTA JONES, I'M NOT AFRAID OF ANYBODY OR ANYTHING! I'M RASTA! YA HEAR ME?" The hollowness of his words fell back on his head like a ton of bricks. Then, this same man, Rasta Jones, who had caused so much destruction, terror and fear, by his name and very presence...balled up his fist, beat his chest and to wailed in hopelessness.

Anzel's descent slowed so dramatically that he began to experience a floating sensation. The strange sounds coming from below were impossible to make out. They began to sound very much like a wounded animal, so much that Anzel shivered in the now warm, stagnant darkness. Gooseflesh rose up and down his arms and legs. Forcing his mind not to dwell on the gruesome possibilities, he tried to recreate the scene on the patio again. What happened? Did he really fall into the earth? He saw himself pacing furiously back and forth, with angry tears dripping, and his heated words came back to him. Shame and self revulsion filled him as he saw his audacity as he tried to read his spiritual resume to The Omnipotent, Omniscient, Omnipresent God of the universe. "Anzel..... Anzel, my son."

The Lord urgently spoke to his heart. "Do not be afraid of what you see and feel in your natural temple. I have created a spiritual connection that you will not be able to understand at this time. Therefore your absolute trusting, obedience is necessary. You are on a rescue mission for the soul of your spiritual brother." Anzel moaned and covered his head with both hands, as the awesomeness of being in the presence of a holy and righteous God, threatened to overwhelm his senses. "Be strong Anzel!" The voice thundered like the rush of many waters. "You are almost in the lion's den. Listen carefully to my instructions, and see that you follow them completely. You will only speak when the Holy Spirit gives you utterance. You must command the spirit of fear to depart from the presence of perfect love. The light that I have placed in you, for such a time as this, will shine brightest in gross darkness." Moaning in pure, holy ecstasy, Anzel managed to ask breathlessly, "Who am I Lord, that You would choose me for this rescue?" Anzel shook helplessly as raw joy saturated every fiber of his being. Then laughter so precious and sweet, surrounded him and drew him into its delightful mirth. When he thought his senses would overload from the fullness of joy, he was released from the sweet agony. He desperately tried to hold onto the words filling his ears, "My love is a vast ocean Anzel, but you must draw on it fully to overcome the evil you are about to come face to face with. I AM THE LORD, I GIVE MERCY TO WHOM I WILL!" "No, Lord don't go!" Anzel cried in a hoarse voice, feeling a piercing loneliness to his very core. Whispers from The Lord returned, swirling all around him, then settling over Anzel like a warm, comfortable blanket. "I will never leave you nor forsake you, beloved, you have My promise......My promise…My prom…"…Anzel fainted.

At Bellview Community Hospital, Ella sat at Dijin's bed-side clutching his hand and studying the tension lines in his dear face. The Doctors had put him in an induced coma to work on bringing his body temperature down. Ella refused to leave his side and politely but firmly brushed off every attempt of the nurses and doctors to send her home. The waiting room was filled to overflowing with family, friends and church members. Ella refused to allow her prayer focus to be interrupted beyond three word responses. She had her petition before Jehovah Raphe, The Healer. She sent her final words to the waiting room, "Just pray." The first time Dijin's eyelids fluttered and he moaned softly, Ella hadn't even waited to push the emergency buzzer. She raced wild eyed into the corridor searching for help. Halfway to the deserted nurse's station she met up with an strikingly beautiful, African American nurse. Ella tried to explain about Dijin in a panicked voice. The nurse patiently explained to Ella that her husband was not coming out of the coma but, that these responses were fairly common as the body settles into its inactive state, and that as long as his vital signs were good, not to worry. Looking into the nurse's eyes, Ella saw nothing but kind concern, and gratefully turned away with a promise not to worry so much. Calling Ella by her first name, the nurse spoke softly, "We both know that Pastor Dijin is in special, infallible hands." She winked at a surprised Ella and walked away quickly. Curiously Ella stared after her wondering who she was. She returned to Dijin's room mildly disturbed. She tried to remember seeing that nurse on the floor before. There had been a soothing, calming effect that her presence had on Ella. How curious. How did she know my name, or that Dijin was a pastor? Being Ella she had to find out. Glancing at a peaceful looking Dijin, Ella left the hospital room to seek out answers to her questions. Approaching the now occupied nurse's station she could see that neither of the two nurses behind the desk was the nurse she had just spoken with. The male nurse was an Asian nurse that had regularly tended to Dijin, while the second nurse was an older, plump Caucasian woman. They looked up curiously at Ella, waiting for her request. Nervously she said, "I want to speak to the young African American nurse who helped me out a few minutes ago." Ella was surprised at the look of confusion on both of their faces. "Mam," the male nurse said with a hint of irritation in his voice. "I know all of the nurses on this shift and I can assure you that there is no African American nurse on the schedule." "Are you sure?" Ella stammered in embarrassment. The second nurse shot a disapproving look at the male nurse's rude response. She answered Ella in a kinder tone. "Yes Mam, we are the only two working this section, do you need anything special?" "Uh no thank you," Ella said feeling like a foolish old lady. She hurried back to the safety of Dijin's hospital room. Leaning her head on his rising and falling chest, she cried fresh tears, her temporary peace gone. "Dijin honey, please come back to me. I don't know what to do here, all alone." The only answer was the clicking and whirring of the various machines helping to keep her husband alive. What Ella was unaware of during her confusion and self pity was that God's sovereign hand was at work in this. Dijin could not rise to consciousness to give Ella the peace of mind she needed by letting her know that he felt no pain or discomfort now. He, himself was just beginning to come into the understanding that the Lord had placed him in this place of solitary confinement, so that his spirit man could pray undisturbed. What or whom he was to pray for, The Lord had not revealed to him yet. He only knew that he had been called to intercession, with an urgency he'd never felt before. And so Dijin Lockhart, pastor, husband, father and spiritual strongman…gave himself over completely to the battle ahead with more than a little spark of anticipation.

Chapter 16

'Choosing Sides'

The sound of Rasta Jones' respirator and various monitors beat in a strange rhythmic pattern that was faintly hypnotic. Secretly spooked, Doctor Tessker quickly checked Rasta's vital signs. He glanced up at the attending nurse and was surprised by her compassionate sigh. The fully armed officer very near the door, refused to look in Rasta's direction. The figure shackled to the bed was definitely a pitiful specimen to the eyes. Even so, Doctor Tessker did not doubt the dangerous nature of the man beast. Still he probably wouldn't last another thirty days unless a miracle occurred. But with God, all things were possible. A question suddenly struck at his heart. "Who is willing to pray for such a man as this?" Where did that come from? "YOU WILL PRAY!" The silent, forceful command settled the question instantly in the doctor's heart. He was a veteran at heart prayers. Working in this profession, he'd had to learn or lose his love of humanity. So while his hands adjusted the various tubes and needles, and while he dictated orders to the nurse, and while the officer at the door, turned a wary eye on the trio across the room...Doctor Maylon Tessker, answered the call of intercession.

Katrina Martinez, bereaved wife of the missing Anzel Martinez tried to ignore the few diehard, reporters milling around, trying to get a shot of her and the twins. For weeks, since Anzel went missing, Katrina's mom had been trying to get her to pack up the girls and move back home. "What if Anzel comes back…and…what if we're not here?" She said in near hysteria. Her mom had finally backed off, looking like she wanted to say so much more to Katrina; instead she'd bitten her bottom lip and turned away. Later she'd grabbed Katrina in a tight bear hug and whispered, "Your dad and I will be praying for you, sweetie, day and night." Hanging up the phone after turning down her parent's hundredth request, she grabbed her hair and gave a mock scream of frustration. The rest of the day, after she and the girls had eaten lunch, she left them with an assortment of their favorite video games and movies. Katrina spent the next two hours looking through family photos, as if they held some clues to this gaping hole in her life. Breaking down she cried out, "Where are you, my love? If I could just hear your voice, touch your face, or smell your skin. Oh God! How can I live with part of my soul missing? ANSWER ME!" She screamed at the ceiling. WHAT DID WE DO TO DESERVE THIS? WE ARE GOOD PEOPLE, WE HAVE DONE NOTHING BUT SERVE YOU, BELIEVE IN YOU….LOVE YOU…..JESUS! YOU'RE GOOD AREN'T YOU, AREN'T YOU?" WHAT DO YOU WANT FROM US? WHY ARE YOU PUNISHING US? WHY?" Angrily turning to walk away, Katrina's eyes fell on her open and neglected bible lying on the dusty coffee table. Bitterly she read the passage in red, "Why call thou me good?" There is none good but God." "NOOOOOOOOO!" Katrina screamed, "THAT'S YOUR ANSWER?" She swept the bible to the floor and tipped over the coffee table. The twins were startled by all the yelling… and they wailed in unison.

Rasta's wails, crystallized into despairing daggers, that ripped mercilessly into his tattered soul. Wounds so deep and numerous that Rasta sagged under the weight of the onslaught. Even on the brink of devastation, Rasta did not dare call on the name of the God of his early childhood. The fear of retaliation from his tormentors kept him petrified like stone. Something was happening to him, he felt himself weakening, growing smaller in ways that he couldn't define. Shivering with deep powerful tremors he wrapped his pencil thin arms around his narrow frame and held on. Was he fading away? How did he feel about the possibility? Wavering between dread and insane glee, a thin sliver of hope began to be born in Rasta's dark heart. Hope? What a strange concept. A mad giggle slipped through Rasta's blackened lips and died in the thick atmosphere. The past words of a fellow inmate flashed instantly through his fried brain. The words crept up and snuffed out the tiny sliver of hope. "All who enter here abandon hope. No hope…no hope….no hope. Wait! What is that? A foot? Now another foot! Now half of a body?" Rasta crashed into the dark surface behind himself, trying to escape from this impossible intrusion. Anzel dropped completely into the small occupied, pit. "You, how did you get in here? Where are we? Is this some kind of sick joke?" Enraged, Rasta snarled, "I'll rip your heart out and eat it before you take your last breath!" Fueled by a supernatural frenzy…he bared his fangs and leapt at Anzel like a rabid dog.

"My promises…The whispers enveloped Anzel, shrouding him like a curious cloak, and although he could see the fierce looking Rasta lunging at him, he seemed to be held back by an invisible leash. Anzel had a powerful feeling of peace all around him. A calm presence dulled the harsh reality of his situation. Familiar words fell softly around him like snowflakes in a Christmas globe. "Let the peace of God, rule in your hearts, to the which, also ye are called in one body, and be ye thankful." He embraced those words, gathering them to his heart, because he was truly thankful. And as the wild figure from his nightmares screeched, snarled and threatened and cursed, Anzel stood silently, in obedience, waiting on the Holy Ghost's command to speak. Finally, exhaustion overcame Rasta and Anzel watched in fascination as the forces driving him berserk, discarded him and he crumpled like a broken rag doll. Anzel felt the barest ember of pity try to ignite in his heart. A question startled him out of his revelry, "Anzel, do you love me?" Filled with anguish, he answered in his heart, "You know I love You Lord." "Feed My lambs." Peace fled from Anzel's heart as regrets and memories of past, missed opportunities to evangelize, flashed before his eyes. "But this man Lord? This dream robber? This blood stealer? Why this brutal animal Lord?" The compassion of The Lord's next words smote Anzel's heart with such a violent force that he was literally slammed to his knees and the air was sucked out of his lungs. "FOR I SO LOVED THE WORLD, THAT I GAVE MY ONLY BEGOTTEN SON, THAT WHOSOEVER BELIEVETH ON HIM SHALL HAVE ETERNAL LIFE!" The words came on a whirlwind, whipping Anzel and Rasta in their intensity. Rasta screamed and tried to shield his face, while Anzel looked into the eye of the storm and feeling the Lord loose his tongue, cried, "Come Lord Jesus, come." Although his screams were lost in the whirlwind, Rasta looked at Anzel with the expression of a trapped animal. "NOOOOooooo! Don't speak that name in this place. You don't know what they're capable of." His eyes darted around fearfully. The wind gathered around Anzel, and to Rasta's terror stricken eyes, he appeared to be consumed by a powerful electrical storm. New eyes shined out of Anzel's face, eyes so full of holy love that Rasta cowered like a whipped puppy. Words began coming out of Anzel's mouth that arrested him and held him captive, searing his skin like acid. Deeper and deeper they went, drilling through Rasta's bones, seeming to separate organs, and piercing him to the very core of his being...it was the power of truth. The gross blackness of Rasta's soul was laid bare before him until death became an longed for escape...Only Rasta couldn't figure out if he were already dead...he sure hoped so.

Katrina was curled up in a ball in Anzel's favorite recliner wrapped in one of his terry cloth bathrobes. The girls were gone to her parent's home for the weekend, and Katrina slept from deep exhaustion and mental and emotional fatigue. She dreamed, and as she dreamed, she smiled as her dream husband whirled her around the dance floor to their favorite love song. It was an original song written by Anzel and his close buddy, Paco Ramirez, who also accompanied him on the keyboard. Anzel was a gifted musician, able to play several instruments as well as sing. Katrina's dimples showed deeply in her sleep. Impossibly, she felt Anzel's warm breath brush her face as he sang the sweet words in her ear. "Lovely dark chocolate, poured into a mold made only for my hands. Lose yourself my lovely lady, in eyes that never tire of your African beauty. In arms that promise to never let you go. We' are one soul, one heartbeat, one life wrapped up together in eternity's embrace. I will never let you go....never let you go...never....Katrina awoke with a start. Her heart was thundering in her chest, and the smell of Anzel's cologne was thick in the room. Looking at her arms, she watched as gooseflesh crept over them. Greedily she drank in the powerful smell of her husband and wept bitterly for her lost lover...who had indeed, let her go.

"Who sent you here?" Rasta yelled into the maelstrom. "Did...they send you here to punish me? I remember you, you were at that school. You saw what we did to that little snitch Wesley." Anzel remained silent, held in check by the holy force of the whirlwind. Wiping the back of his filthy hand across his mouth, Rasta spat contemptuously at Anzel's feet. Cruelly eyeing him he said, "Yeah, we took care of little Wesley, we fixed him up real good. I fixed you some too, huh? Put my little ownership tag on you. My little initiation bite on your arm, yeah, made you my special, blood brother." Rasta cracked up at his own sick humor. Anzel continued to watch Rasta while he waited to see what was required of him next. "Not yet, the time is coming." The words brushed softly against his ears. Anzel's impatience eased as he waited on the Lord. So Anzel waited and Rasta cursed, and blasphemed...meanwhile the marker was being called in for Rasta's soul.

In the spiritual realm, a segment of the heavenly host faced off against a portion of the legions of darkness. The angels of light stood silent, foreboding, strikingly beautiful, and seemingly oblivious to the seething, repulsive mass hurling threats and insults in their direction. Their instructions did not allow them to acknowledge the filthy horde until they would be ordered to strike them down. These huge, regal beings stood in perfect formation, with their very presence causing rage, fear and panic in the filthy, putrid ranks of their enemies. Turning on each other in frustrated fury, the horde clawed and gashed each other until they created a thick wall of noxious vapors. Impenetrable, the heavenly army shimmered in righteous indignation. Screeching in agony, the hideous creatures attacked each other more ferociously. Ripping, gouging and tearing into their comrades. Crushing heads, eyes, anything they could reach...They raged in pain and insane blood lust against an unmovable barrier.

Secure in the whirlwind, Anzel rested as his longing for Katrina and his girls, Kiamara and Asharia, felt tangible, but held safely in limbo. Something was growing in Anzel's heart. It was something foreign and slightly alarming. The more he studied the creature that was Rasta Jones his anger was being squeezed out of existence. His inability to forgive was being crowded out by a powerful wave of compassion and the knowledge that Jesus Christ's redeeming love, paid for it all on the cross. Anzel, rocked upright against the power of God's love towards the pitiful creature before him. Finally, released from the prison of hatred and unforgiveness, Anzel exulted in his new found freedom. The knowledge of his son ship and inheritance in eternal glory became a thick, protective shield all around him. The light of God's love burst out of Anzel,... he just couldn't contain it.

The second shift doctor and two nurses stood looking at each other through the opening of their protective masks. The masks covered mouths set with either pity or disgust. Bound by their Hippocratic Oath, they would do everything that was possible to help the pathetic creature, writhing in agony on the fouled hospital bed. The resident on duty, Doctor Andrew Woods, walked a short distance away from the bed and the sad action to look over Rasta's lengthy medical history. Shaking his head, he stared at the condensed records of twelve years of Human Immunodeficiency Virus Infection. Rumors of how Rasta first contracted the HIV infection crushed the tiny spark of compassion he had previously felt towards this dark, soulless creature. Unconsciously he made the sign of the cross. The information presented before him was incredible. How had this man survived, especially with the limited medications and treatments available in the many institutions that housed him over the years? "Ah!" He exclaimed, as he read along further. Rasta was the recipient of a number of experimental drugs and procedures. He read on, two viral infections, Cytomegalovirus and Herpes Simplex Virus. A parasitic infection called Toxoplasma Gondil Neoplasms, Nonhodgekins Lymphoma and Broncogenic Carcinoma, along with a host of other symptoms. Hmmm, oh yes, of course, mouth sores, how ironic! He thought dryly. The patient had suffered a bout of Dermatitus, and at present his CD4 cell count was at fifty cells/FL. Also they were presently dealing with M. Avium Complex, Nonendemic Fungi and Aspergillus Candida. One thing Doctor Woods was positive of, all of these hundred dollar words added up to one conclusion, a brutal ending to a brutal life. He felt a small, very tiny stirring of pity. Maybe he had some humanity left after all. "Doctor Woods? Doctor Woods"...He dropped the papers and ran to join the pointless, lifesaving efforts.

Chapter 17

'Survival Instincts'

Katrina Martinez eased her worn, aching limbs into the soapy, super heated hot tub. She had begged Anzel to have it installed for their third wedding anniversary. He had balked at the cost for a while, and held out against Katrina's feminine wiles for as long as he was able, but Katrina just about eyelash batted and dimpled him to death. In the end, Anzel ended up using it as much as Katrina. Her mind battled against her body as she refused to let the pleasure of the hot, soapy water overshadow her sorrow and loss. But when the steamy, bubbly water rushed over her tension strained muscles, an involuntary sigh of delight escaped her lips. Five minutes later mental fatigue won out and she drifted away on cloud of vanilla scented bubbles. "Chicka?" Katrina's eyelids fluttered. "Chicka?" Warm breath whispered against her cheek like a gentle kiss. Half asleep, she smiled in contentment and lifted a soapy hand to the side of her face. "Yes babe? Yes my love? Anzel?" She came violently awake with her heart hammering in her chest. She looked wildly around the bathroom for Anzel. She had expected him to be perched on the side of the tub as usual with a mischievous grin on his face. Reality slammed into her with the force of a semi truck, leaving her screaming in rage against an unseen attacker. Shaken and sobbing, she crawled, broken and defeated out of the hot tub, unwilling to feel anything close to relief now. Only when the chilly air became too much, did she cover her shivering frame with Anzel's terry cloth robe, and a blanket of hopelessness. Passing in front of the slightly steamed vanity mirror, Katrina stopped short and stared at the haggard face of the stranger looking back at her. The beautiful, hazel eyes were haunted, reflecting deep pools of suffering. The delicate features were drawn with bitterness. Reaching a trembling hand towards the mirror, she shrieked at the fact that she was the pitiful creature trapped in the glass. With a strangled sob, she fled from the bathroom, the truth pursuing, close on her heels. She wasn't over Anzel's disappearance... and she wondered if she would ever, ever be.

Pastor Dijin Lockhart was floating, weightless, unafraid and for the first time in his entire Christian career, he was totally submitted to the will of God. He had no memory of how he came to be in this condition, he was only aware of an intense burden of prayer for Anzel Martinez, his wife, the female stranger from another time and the animal like man. Dijin burned with a singleness of holy purpose. God was truly the author of these events and Dijin wanted to see what end He had in store for His children. The words, *The Thinning*, whispered around his head, softly caressing his face. Dijin wept unashamedly, in this silent cocoon. Huge wracking sobs shook his weightless form. "Dijin? Do you love me?" The voice spoke urgently, irresistibly. He could only nod his tearstained face, and continue the broken hearted sobs. "Do you want to see what real love looks like?" Frozen in place by the realization of Who it was communicating with him, caused his body to shake with inhuman joy. "Keep praying, dear child and remember my words, *"The effectual, fervent prayers of a righteous man, availeth much."*...So Pastor Dijin Lockhart, alternated between heart wrenching sobs, passionate prayers and mind numbing bliss.

Doctor Pila Thomas, fully succumbed, to the exhaustion that overtook her mind and she dreamed. She was cradling Ryia's head in her blood soaked lap. Ryia's face was frozen in a hideous grimace of pained surprise. Pila started wailing and calling her sister's name, "Ryia, Ryia!" Suddenly someone stepped out from behind the rubber trees directly behind the irrigation ditch... Rasta! The Rag tree Man! Pila blanched and stumbled backwards, dragging Ryia's lifeless body with her. Feeling herself falling, she looked up expecting Rasta to be almost on top of them. Instead she watched in horror as Rasta, eyes went wide with terror, as he burst into flames... The sound of his screams followed Pila into the land of blessed wakefulness.

Clasping her trembling hands around her fourth cup of espresso, Pila tried to analyze the meaning of the dreams. What possible connection could Rasta have had with her sister's death? Ryia had died many years before Rasta was even born, and many more miles. This mystery was beginning to cause Pila to unravel. It was a mystery indeed. What in land sakes was she dealing with here? Something tugged at the edges of her memory. There was something from her days in university? Pila curled a lock of her hair around her index finger and gently pulled. This was a memory exercise that she had developed for her Alzheimer's patients. She focused her thoughts on the gentle pulling rhythm and the sealed door to her memory began to unlock. She had recorded a 25 percent success rate with her early stage patients. It was coming back to her. Her senior year in graduate school there were a group of professors that were all a buzz over a term paper written by a student at a nearby seminary. The student had written about a bizarre sect of monks or priests, she thought. What was the topic of the paper? Something to do with a forbidden practice, she tugged at her hair a little harder, ouch! yes that was it. A practice called Training? No, that didn't sound right. One more yank on her tender hair. I got it, Troaning. It was the practice of thinning one's existence for a single, set purpose, while living on the barest of necessities and focusing on a common goal. If her memory served her well, some of the priest lost their lives trying to mentally break through some crystallite cubes or blocks. "This is totally insane." She muttered. But what this had to do with the Rasta or Ryia situation was not clear at all. Pila's survival instincts stirred. It wasn't by happenstance that she had survived the tragic deaths of her parents and only sibling. That she'd mastered loneliness and the bitterness of divorce. Doctor Pila Thomas wasn't used to staying under. No she would get to the bottom of this mystery, and she would do it Pila style…She owed it to Ryia's memory.

Pila's return to sleep, two hours later, threw her right back into her vulnerable state as a player in her own dreams. This time bits and pieces of quilted squares of her dream were weaving together, and then shattering into bizarre collages. First, she was back at the prison looking through the Plexiglas in confusion at a shackled, cursing, spitting Anzel Martinez.

Then she was falling down a long, dark hole, and all around her, she could hear screams of agony and cries of hopelessness. Now back on her childhood plantation in Sri Llenka, but instead of cradling the bloody form of her sister, she was holding a dead, bloody Katrina Martinez. Stroking the blood soaked hair away her face, Pila's tears washed her, as she tearfully whispered over and over again, "hold on Katrina, help is coming. Hold on Katrina, help is coming, hold on"...Pila came awake with a start. "Katrina?"There was a urgency in the atmosphere, Katrina was in some kind of trouble. Pila reached for her eyeglasses and glanced at her digital clock on the nightstand. "Four o'clock in the morning? What am I supposed to do at this ungodly hour? What does that mean anyway? I cannot go barging into someone's home at this hour, telling them I had a dream about them."The feeling of urgency filled Pila, and she chased her usual logical rebuttal up the nearest tree. Pila almost burst out laughing from sheer fright as her cell phone chirped, the second she reached for it. The smile died on her lips as a desperate whisper came through the phone. "I don't think I can go on like this!" "Katrina?" Pila said carefully. "Doctor Thomas?" Katrina's voice crackled with emotion. "I can't keep hurting like this, I can't live without Anzel!" Pila's professional side kicked into gear. "Mrs. Martinez, are you standing or sitting?" A hesitant, "standing." Katrina sounded suspicious, good, that was a sign of self preservation. "Katrina, are you alone?Who is caring for those beautiful girls of yours?" "Uh, yes, my girls are with their grandparents...I'm...all... alone." Pila was startled by the emphasis that Katrina put on the word, alone. She chose he next moves carefully, knowing that they would be crucial to the outcome of this tragic situation. Pila may have failed Wesley and Anzel, but she would fight to the death for Katrina Martinez...Her only questions were, fight who, and with what?

Ella started from her thoughts when the sound of Dijin moaning broke through a veil of self pity. His brows were tightly knit together as if there were a struggle going on inside of him. Beads of perspiration broke out on his forehead. Ella looked frantically around as several monitors began to react noisily. Her eyes flew back and forth from the emergency button to the door. She was halfway out of her chair when the machines stopped their beeping and Dijin released a long sigh and his facial features relaxed. Dear God, what was going on here? Glancing at her wristwatch she noted the early hour. Ella's heart filled with fear, and reaching for Dijin's hand she held on tightly...and glared at the monitor's daring them to go off again.

Katrina sat on the side of her bed tightly clutching a small bottle of sleeping pills. She couldn't even remember where or why she had gotten them. Heavily sighing, she realized that she had forgotten to get a cup of water to help swallow them. She almost smiled at her own forgetfulness. Anzel used to tease her by saying, "Chicka, girl, if you didn't have me around you would probably fall into a ditch." Well, she didn't have him now, she felt like she had been swallowed into a ditch whole. What did she forget, to bring on this kind of suffering? How foolish to overlook water to help take an overdose of pills. Well who was an expert at killing one's self? There, she'd formed the words and she'd faced what it was that she was going to do. But why had she called Doctor Thomas? She'd had an irresistible urge to dial her number. Certainly the girls would hurt for a time, but they were young and with her parents love and support they would move on. It was better this way. What was the use? She couldn't even pray to a God she wouldn't trust, ever again. "What about it God?" Rage ripped through her chest. Don't You care about us? Well, You know what? You had Job, why did you need to make me lose Anzel? You can't hurt me anymore"…her voice trailed off. Wearily she said, "I'm not going to argue with you anymore, I don't have the strength to fight anymore, I'm just going to take these pills and lie down on Anzel's side of the bed and wait to stop feeling….anything. She growled with frustration as she remembered that she could not dry swallow a hand full of pills. She didn't want to choke to death. Mentally, she measured the distance from her bed to the bathroom sink. Hysterical laughter spewed out of her cotton dry mouth as she thought about the bitter irony of it. She was too depressed to kill herself. How ridiculous was that? Forcing herself to a standing position, by sheer will, she took a few steps and her slipper caught under the corner of the room sized rug and the pills fell harmlessly to the floor, rolling under her dresser drawers. Katrina felt an annoyed surprise as she saw herself falling in slow motion. Her right temple struck the edge of the nightstand. After a blinding jolt of pain, instant darkness rushed up to meet her. Katrina knew she was screaming because her mouth and eyes were stretched wide open, only there was no sound and only unyielding blackness. Sightless and soundless, she dropped, her fall unbroken. A wave of fear, she had never experienced before, filled her entire being. Suddenly, she sensed that she was not alone. Clawed, hands reached out of the darkness and covered her silent screams. Foul, scaly fingers worked their way into her mouth and down her throat. Katrina tried to gag violently, but the clawed fingers continued moving down her throat. Her air supply was completely cut off as she bucked and kicked wildly, but to no avail. Gabbing at her neck desperately, pain and terror struggled for first place in her mind. Other claws began to reach out for her. They tore and stabbed as they mercilessly ripped her tender flesh. All of this horror was accompanied by cold, hideous laughter, which played inside her head. Just when Katrina thought that blessed nothingness would rescue her from the violence against her, the attacks would intensify. Continuously hovering near unconsciousness, she now, knew that she would be forever denied any relief. Because, this surely must be hell. Was there anything worse than this? That's when the horrific burning of her remaining flesh began…From the souls of her feet to the crown of her head, moving one agonizing inch at a time, the fire crawled over her mauled body.

Chapter 18
'Weapons of Warfare'

Rasta was severely smitten in the face of God's love pouring from Anzel's face and streaming from his hands. The demons in Rasta, screamed in rage and agony trying to flee this small taste of their anguish to come. Scenes from Rasta's life began to appear in the heavenly light. Rasta at five years old, begging his mother not to leave him. Rasta could feel the helpless anger, the rage, as the dark enemies within him seethed in hatred. Even though Rasta was afraid he would be torn in two, he enjoyed exquisite satisfaction at his tormentor's fear. A tiny dot of hope poked through Rasta's consciousness, so he held onto the tiny speck with the instincts of a dying beast. The light from Anzel burned brighter, searing Rasta. Dazed, he looked around, hearing music so sweet that it washed over his dead, senses in pure melodious waves. His legs collapsed under his weight and he sprawled on his hands and knees before the glory emanating from Anzel. "GET UP YOU FOOL!" The voices shrieked in Rasta's ears. Rasta tried to obey, but he could only kneel and sob brokenly, despising his weakness, but helpless to change his circumstances. Other voices in the distance captured Rasta's attention. As Anzel's light began to dim he could see a fiery darkness approaching. "Doctor, were losing him!" "Nurse, bring that crash cart closer!" "He's flat lining!" "Okay we've got a faint pulse. It's very weak but it's there." Where were those voices coming from? Were they talking about him?

Rasta? How could that be? Suddenly there was screaming coming from the darkness. Not physical voices, but a crescendo of human emotions desperately rushing towards the lesser darkness. It clawed at Rasta's very essence for release. Rasta's soul recoiled from the onslaught of suffering and anguish. He was able to distinguish voices now. Words took shape, in horrible, fiery letters that danced and writhed in the air as though written by an invisible finger. Rasta thought he would dissolve from fear as he read the hellish message. *"Times up Rasta, you belong in here with us! We will have our desire upon you brother, forever!!!!"* Then laughter so evil, that the peals of it ripped at Rasta's skin and filled the air. "NOOooooo!" Rasta whimpered, too afraid to feel ashamed as his bowels broke loose. Rasta was torn between two worlds, two horrible realms where pain and fear reigned as king...and there was...no...way...out.

Praying intensely for Dijin's quick recuperation, Ella was vaguely aware of a commotion in the corridor. Hearing the sound of running feet and wheels accompanied by panicked voices, she offered up an quick distracted prayer, "Lord, please bless that poor soul in distress, in Jesus name Amen.....There was no way for her to know the role that she and her husband were to play in the outcome of that commotion.

Pila threw down her green, crocodile New Yorker bag and ground her teeth in frustration. How could she not find her car keys? They were the very same keys that she always, always kept on the peg by the front door. So that she could grab them in a moment's notice. Every since the catastrophe of nineteen eighty four, when she was almost late to her own wedding. Oh, well maybe that wasn't a good example because she wished she hadn't shown up at all. To add insult to injury, her cell phone died just when she was attempting to contact Katrina's parents to let them know that their daughter was in some kind of trouble. Determined to get to Katrina, Pila overlooked the distance that she had moved her potted cactus away from its corner perch. Down she went in a flurry of wildly swinging arms and legs. Now what had she gotten herself into, she wondered. She looked up at the ceiling and rubbed the rising bump just shy of the crown on her head...One of the Hindu statues that adorned her coffee table, grinned mockingly at her clumsiness.

Dijin was no longer floating peacefully. He was falling at an alarming rate. An unspoken urgency surged through his entire being. "Get Katrina Martinez!" His whole reason for existing was pinpointed for this moment. Nothing else mattered to him. A commanding voice, with the sound of rushing waters spoke. Everything within Dijin collapsed in the presence of the most powerful love of all times and times to come. "Servant, look neither to your left, your right nor behind you. Do not speak, nor give indication to your enemies that you have heard their accusations, or threats. For The Lord is your refuge, your very present help in the time of trouble." Dijin was locked in such a rictus of joy and ecstasy, that he felt he would gladly perish in the throes of God's love. Just as he approached the end of his endurance, the light withdrew and Dijin's spirit expelled a mournful sigh of intense longing and sorrow. The feelings faded enough for Dijin to face the task at hand, and he set himself to get Katrina. He was confident that God would take care of the details...And so he fell into the darkness, unaware of the light's intense reflection which compassed him completely.

Katrina struggled to make sense of the agony that was her entire existence now. Even as she tried to turn inside of herself, terrible pictures of her hidden sins and wicked thoughts were there to expose her. A heavy cloak of condemnation coiled tightly around her middle, cutting off any crumbs of hope to be grabbed for. If she could cry out, she would beg for mercy, but hadn't she lost her chance? Instinctively she knew that there would never be mercy in this place. She would cry out for a tiny drop of water on her tongue to slake the agony of her thirst. But surely there was no water in this hellish nightmare. She would plead for the fire to stop burning her, or to consume her completely. She would scream for someone, anyone, to remove the worms that were crawling in and out of every opening of her body. Somebody, to please stop the beatings that left her feeling like every bone in her body was being smashed over and over again. And the laughter inside of her head. The cold, hideous shrieks, every time a blow was struck. Her broken and smashed arms hung useless from dislocated shoulders, while her crushed skull, jerked forward as the abuse continued, uninterrupted. Suddenly a thought, more cruel and hideous than all of the torture that Katrina had endured so far entered her mind. It was a thought that was more frightening than the flames that engulfed her. A thought that pierced her broken heart, she, Katrina Jewel Brewster, Martinez...did...not...have to be in this God forsaken place.

"Got them!" Pila held her car keys triumphantly over her head. Grabbing the wrong jacket for the unseasonably warm morning, she rushed into the garage. With one arm in the sleeve and her fully charged cell phone on speed dial, she jumped into her green Honda Civic, and barely allowed the garage door to clear before she pulled under it. A groggy male voice that Pila assumed was Katrina's dad answered warily. She quickly explained her conversation with Katrina. She hurriedly gave them assurance that she would be calling them in approximately thirty minutes with news. She bit back a flippant remark as Katrina's father promised her that they would be fervently praying for their daughter. Smiling in bewilderment, Pila shook her head. These Christians were relentless. Exactly twenty nine minutes later she was parking her car across the street from Anzel and Katrina's, neat, Tudor style home. It was really a beautiful, manicured home, but for some reason, it cast a dark foreboding shadow, which spilled onto the street, and almost appeared to be reaching for Pila's car. The tiny hairs on the back of Pila's neck stood up as goose flesh broke out on her sleeveless arm. Absently touching the newest knot on her head, she repeated the question she'd asked herself earlier… "What have you gotten yourself into now?"

Katrina sensed something coming. She could not see or hear beyond her evil situation, but she felt a sudden flurry of fearful activity begin to ripple the painful darkness. The shrieks took on a different quality, as if the pain and suffering was being shared by her tormentors. There was a fleeing away of darkness, a ripping and tearing of the gross blackness. The minutest, lessoning of agony, and Katrina latched onto it. Dijin refused to feed his horrible curiosity and turn to look at the hideous things that began to emerge out of the darkness. They raged in hatred at this intrusion of light into their dark realm. The knowledge that they had no power to utterly destroy this interrupter drove them to the brink of insanity. Dijin fought the desire to shrink away from the intensity of their hatred, but the words of The Father, burned in his breast. They were a shield when the vile accusations and threats and humiliating images of his sins were hurled at him. Pictures of his shameful past were laid open and exposed to the cruelest ridicule. The darkest secrets of his heart, held up to sadistic mirth and slanderer's glee. "The Lord is my refuge." Those words returned and pierced through the wicked onslaught, railing against his mind. Peering into the darkness with renewed courage, he could see the top of a head. The closer he got, he was able to recognize that it was Katrina. It was the battered, barely recognizable Katrina Martinez. Dijin recoiled, even as his heart squeezed with profound pity. Feeling the guidance of The Holy Ghost, Dijin leaned over and reached into the swirling, viscose darkness and with both hands, lifted the pitiful, broken form, even while foul, cursing, slashing demons, clung to the broken, distorted legs. When the light compassing Dijin, came into contact with the foul, filthy imps, they burst asunder, screeching, as their putrid pieces fell deeper into the fiery darkness. Katrina Martinez lay unmoving, with bloody eyes, staring sightlessly into the light. Dijin startled when the sound of an inhuman wail assaulted his ears. It was a moment before he realized that the wail was coming from his own lips...Even more frightening was the fact that he didn't know if he could stop it.

The majestic, heavenly army cheered and waved swords victoriously in the air at the defeat of the enemy horde. They had been given their orders in one powerful word, "Now!"

With unrestrained glee they had turned and crushed the enemies of the Christ. They were allowed to release all of their pent up indignation until Katrina Martinez was completely out of the enemy's grasp...Satisfaction and joy, abounded.

Chapter 19
'His Insatiable Love'

Rasta's crumpled form became painfully erect as a charge lit the cramped atmosphere. A loud popping sound followed by the pungent smell of lilacs filled his senses. The fear and agony coursing through him began to retreat from these newest developments. Something was going on right outside of his eye and earshot. He could tell that it was something important and that it concerned his unwell being. Whatever it was, it was causing him to go on the defensive. He watched Anzel through narrowly slit eyelids as he absently licked at a cracked and bleeding lip. The taste of the blood sent fresh fury through his thoughts, leaving him desperately confused. Icy fingers of fear returned and began to tighten around his painfully constricting heart. Could he survive this kind of terror? He had to give out soon, or was this the beginning of the end? Pushing at his heaving chest with thin, filthy hands, Rasta tried to quiet the thunderstorm behind his breastbone because Anzel was speaking to him now. Vainly he tried to reign in the forces fighting to keep him captive from Anzel's words. With wide panicked eyes he gaped as fire began to stream from between Anzel's lips. Anzel's eyes glowed with a pure, bluish, white energy, and the brightness seared Rasta's retinas. Every word that was spoken to him brought the piercing blue, white light close to his chest. Shrinking away in amazement, Rasta began to listen to the voice of fire. The intensity of the energy threatened to consume Rasta and his thundering heart. When Rasta felt himself giving up the tiny life left in him, the light began to dim and withdraw. Was that disappointment that briefly flashed across Anzel's face? Speaking in a curiously calm tone Anzel continued telling a story. He appeared totally indifferent to the suffering man now. Saul? Who is Saul? Rasta spat scornfully. Never losing the steady flow of words Anzel said, "Saul was a man who was greatly feared by the Jews, because he made it his business to bring punishment and suffering to the people of God." Helplessly, Rasta squirmed, trapped like an insect on the end of a pin…Forced to listen to the ranting of this fanatical, Jesus freak.

In the Intensive Care Unit at Bellview Community Hospital, medical staff worked frantically on the dying body of Rasta Jones. The only sounds in the room were hurried instructions and labored breathing. Suddenly, to the shock and bewilderment of the doctors and nurses on the emergency team, Rasta's vital signs began to return to normal. One slightly cynical nurse, later made this remark to a group of her peers, in the cafeteria…"Rasta Jones either has nine lives or he sold his soul to the devil." Wisely, no one responded.

As Anzel relentlessly continued ahead in his storytelling, the demon spirits inside of Rasta fled in terror. Two luminescent hands reached inside of Rasta and lifted his terrified spirit from his body. Rasta's yell of surprise died in his throat as he watched his battered, disease ridden body collaspe like a pile of dirty rags. He was then slammed into a wall of flesh and bone. Dazed, he squinted up into a blinding light and felt the intense heat of the sun on his face. His face tingled from drying perspiration. He ran his unfamiliar tongue over his unfamiliar, cracked lips. Raging hatred filled him with an evil purpose. This hatred did not come from his usual stockpile, but it was directed towards the followers of Jesus Christ. He breathed threats and murder against them as he put it into action. The next few seconds revealed to Rasta, that somehow he had become the man in Anzel's story, The Apostle Paul, who was still Saul at this point in the story. Whoa! What? How? He was Saul of Tarsus and he was on his way to Damascus. With this knowledge, he felt a shifting and he became one with this stranger. Before he could grow accustomed to this insanity, he heard a voice coming from the light, "Saul, Saul, why are you persecuting Me?" The lips parted without his bidding and he answered, "Who are you Lord?" Freezing inside with terror in the presence of holiness, he trembled at the answer. "I am Jesus, whom you are persecuting. It is hard for you to kick against the goads." Before Rasta could form any response, he was quickly lifted out of Saul and literally dropped back into his own ragged looking shell. The demonic spirits greeted him with scathing insults and leapt upon him with vicious glee. Anzel continued the story with great animation, seeing that he had Rasta's full attention now. His total fascination, allowed Rasta to ignore the abusive demons as if they were common household flies. Time after time, as he listened to Anzel's accounts, he was transported as an unwilling participant into the story of Apostle Paul's life. The next trip, he is Saul, experiencing the terror of blindness. Another time he is hidden in a basket, heart thudding in his chest, while being lowered over a wall, trying to escape a death plot. Every time that Rasta was returned to his own body, Anzel would be speaking in an uninterrupted flow. Rasta, as Paul in Lystra, commanding a man, crippled from his mother's womb, "Stand up straight on your feet!" Even as the young man began to leap on his feet, Rasta was jerked back into his own shell. Disappointment startled him. On and on it continued. Rasta had no idea how long, because time did not seem to exist in this place. Something was altering inside of Rasta's heart. Each time he returned from being knit with the body and spirit of the Apostle Paul, he felt as if the things in his heart were a little less painful. There was a shaving away of the black rage that was so much a part of him. Anzel fixed Rasta with an intense stare and raised his voice to a deafening level. Rasta willed his weak, pencil thin arms to lift up and cover his ears, but they refused to obey him. The demonic spirits cowered and threw empty threats at Rasta, realizing that their hold on him was quickly diminishing. A look of profound compassion followed Rasta as he was being pulled from his body, yet again. Before he could sneer at Anzel's pity, he was lifting Paul's head and feeling the agony of forty stripes, minus one on his naked back. Rasta screamed as his poorly circulated hands strained against the leather straps. His arms were pulled to the limit, almost dislocating his shoulders. Barely conscious he knew that there had been a trial, and that as Paul, he had been threatened to obey the command not to preach the gospel, he also knew as Paul, that it would be easier to refuse the air he breathed, than to give up the heart fire that drove him relentlessly through the nations of the earth. How could he not spread the hope of glory? Not share the message of the resurrected Savior? Impossible! As Apostle Paul, he knew that he was willing to die for this heart fire. For the first time in his life, Rasta had a full understanding of who Jesus Christ was. The Son of The Living God. The Only

real Redeemer. The Father, Son and Holy Ghost. So many unfamiliar words crowded Rasta's warring mind. Rabbi, Healer,
Savior, Shepherd. Rasta was yanked back and he was angry this
time. Anzel was taken aback at the passion in Rasta's eyes…He
continued the story, helpless to stop.

Chapter 20

'Let the Redeemed Say So'

Stepping up and admiring the sculptured, oak door gracing the front of the Martinez home, Pila neglected to notice a tangled pair of jump ropes and almost went down on the cobblestone walkway. Looking around sheepishly, she scolded herself for the zillionth time, about her klutzy feet. The beautiful home had such an ominous feel about it. By habit, Pila struggled to put her feelings into logical, descriptive terms. This was one of her more effective therapy tactics. The house, she decided was like a beautiful shell, devoid of any life, or warmth. "Stop it Pila!" She fussed at herself, "you are getting maudlin in your old age." Reaching out to ring the doorbell, she found that her hand was shaking violently. She glared at it, accusingly. Silently, she willed it to be still. Several minutes with no response to her ringing, Pila tried the doorknob, and to her dismay, it opened. Not a good sign. Nervously glancing over her shoulder, she stepped quickly inside and softly shut the door. The sharp twerp of her cell phone scared her and she banged the back of her already tender head against the hard oak door. Muttering in her native tongue, she rolled her eyes at the now silent phone, and put it on vibrate without looking at the caller ID. PPT kicked in, personal protection training. Pila moved through the dim living room area, with her body constantly turning at forty five degree angles. She kept her cell phone tucked towards her body, with it set for nine eleven speed dial. She also carried her combination, flashlight, pepper spray, slash whistle tucked closely to her body. Having checked each room on the first floor, she warily eyed the stairs to the second level. Quickly scaling them, she paused at the top step as her eyes spotted light spilling from what looked like a master bedroom. Feeling the hair rise on the back of her neck, Pila forced herself to check the other rooms on the floor. Reluctantly, Pila returned to the first room. She heard a heavy thump as if something heavy had fallen. Reaching for the doorknob, she froze in fear, when she was greeted with a blood curdling scream. In all of Pila's years working with the emotionally disturbed, the criminally corrupt and those who suffered at the hands of her patients, she had never heard the caliber of fear that was coming from behind that door. Feeling her knees crash together and grabbing onto the knob, caused the door to swing open and spill Pila right into the storm of screams. Teeth chattering loudly, she asked herself…"PPPila, what… hhhhhave… yyyyou… gggggotten… yyyyourself… iiiiiinto… nnnnnow?"

Katrina Martinez, lay face up on the bedroom floor with half of her body hidden underneath the bed. Someone was screaming so loud that she thought her eardrums would burst. Oh God someone please help that poor soul. Who ever she might be. Something terrible must have happened to her. Her returning sight showed her a shocked, openmouthed Doctor Thomas trying to recover her balance, in her bedroom doorway. Thank God the screaming had stopped. Blinking her eyes against the light she painfully struggled to sit up and realized that she was partially under her bed. Opening her mouth to ask Pila why she had run into her bedroom, her voice croaked out in a barely audible whisper. Panicking,, she clawed wildly at her throat as memories began to assault her. A look of deep distress came over Katrina's face and using both of her feet she back pedaled into the wall behind her. Rolling over onto her side, she curled up into the fetal position and alternated between whimpers and hiccups. Rarely was Doctor Pila Thomas at a loss for words, but as she stood frozen in the doorway, looking at the bruised and battered form, cowering in terror, all she could do rub the swelling lump on her head, as the words whispered through her mind…"The Rag tree man's gonna get you, run, Rasta's gonna get you."

Pastor Dijin Lockhart's fever broke at the exact moment that Pila was exiting her car outside the Martinez's home. Just seconds before it broke, Ella had lost her battle with fatigue, at his bedside. She almost jumped out of her skin because of a loud yelp from her previously comatose husband. Ella's startled eyes met the wild, terrified eyes of Dijin. Frantic, Ella grabbed for the call button on the hospital bed, and almost collided with Dijin as he struggled to untangle himself from cords, tubes and bedding. "Dijin, sweetheart please lay back before you hurt yourself." "Ella, oh Ella, it's so good to see you." Dijin rasped. Croaking at Ella with urgency he rushed on, "Ella, we have to leave here, now. Please, there's a urgency in my spirit." Dijin was overcome by a coughing spell. Ella turned and grabbed the water pitcher from the bedside table and filled up an empty cup. Dijin smiled weakly, and gulped down six cups of the lukewarm water before his thirst was quenched. Ella placed her hands firmly on Dijin's shoulders, pressing him down to have her say. ""Now you listen to me you stubborn, old coot." Dijin looked at Ella, taken aback. "You will not leave this hospital until the doctor declares you fully well, and releases you." Dijin broke out into a broad grin, purposely making his eyes, crinkle at the corners. "Don't you dare try to work your Irish charm on me I've been married to you for too many years to fall for that old gimmick." Running his tongue over his parched lips, his grin turned sheepish as he realized that his dentures were absent. Ella tried not to let Dijin see the smirk on her face. Sobering up suddenly, she said, "Okay, sweetheart, all kidding aside, Dij, where have you been? You left me here all alone, and I was so scared that I was going to lose you." Seeing the stark relief in her eyes, he bit off the humorous remark on the tip of his tongue, and grabbed both of Ella's hands, as he tried to think of a way to explain what he himself did not fully comprehend. He knew that he had been in the presence of The Holy God of Abraham, Isaac, Jacob and Dijin. It was in a way that he would have never imagined could be possible. He had heard God's direction clearer than ever before and was successful in his assignment. Wow! Awesome! Scary! Fantastic! How do you tell your wife that you visited, and rescued someone from the very outskirts of hell? And lived and returned to tell about it? Most likely the memories would haunt Dijin for the rest of his natural life. And Katrina, poor Katrina, Katrina? Dijin bolted upright suddenly, scaring Ella. "Ella, you've got to get me out of here. Katrina Martinez, I need to know what has come of Katrina. I had her right in my arms! Then poof!" Confused, Ella reached for her husband's frail hand and tried to comfort him. "Dij, honey, that's impossible I was right here by your side all the time." Seeming not to hear her, Dijin excitedly continued, "Oh Ella, she was so… so…she was", then to Ella's utter amazement, her husband burst out crying. Reaching for him, she folded his large frame in a tight embrace and crooned assurance in the singsong voice she had used with their children. She patted his broad back an allowed him to release himself in this floodgate of tears. There would be plenty of time later to get an explanation. Although, they would not be leaving Bellview Community Hospital until she knew as much as Dijin was not telling. Seeing Ella's set face, Dijin sighed in resignation, knowing enough about his soul mate to understand, that she would have her way and she would get it in a godly manner. Clearing his throat, he gave Ella a condensed version. As he came to the end of his astounding tale, Ella with a pale resigned face, helped Dijin to sit completely upright…and resolved herself to face the confrontation with the hospital for her husband's immediate release.

Anzel's voice faded as Rasta was placed gently this time into the body of Paul the Aged. He is imprisoned and feeling the bite of winter and the sting of being deserted by friends, whom he loves. Rasta quickly identifies with the loneliness in Paul's heart, but feels confusion at the peace that overshadows it. Knowledge from Paul fills Rasta. The demonic cruelty of Emperor Nero, who blames Christians for burning down Rome, and has in turn, exacted a horrific campaign of torture and executions. Rasta as Paul blows warm breath on his swollen, arthritic knuckles as he shivers from the brutal cold. Rasta's eyes fall on the letter Paul is in the process of writing. He is addressing a letter to his beloved spiritual son, Timothy. The concept of loving a son who is not of your blood is totally foreign to Rasta. Startled, Rasta feels Paul's certainty that this will be his final communication, because his departure is near. "Death!" Rasta wants to say to Paul, "Why are you wasting time writing trying to send comforting words to this man who is no relation to you, when you are about to die?" His thoughts are silenced as Paul writes, *"Therefore I endure all things for the sake of the elect, that they also may obtain the salvation which is in Christ Jesus with eternal glory."* Curious as to the meaning of Paul's words, he watches as he shares in Paul's writing. *"This is a faithful saying: for if we die with Him, we shall also live with Him. If we endure, we shall also reign with Him, if we deny Him, He will also deny us. If we are faithless, He remains faithful; He cannot deny Himself."* Deeply troubled, Rasta mourns his own life, which was a complete denial of Jesus Christ. An alien feeling of admiration fills Rasta at Paul's next thoughts, they write, *"For I am being poured out as a drink offering, and the time of my departure is at hand. I have fought the good fight, I have finished the race, I have kept the faith. Finally there is laid up for me, the crown of righteousness, which The Lord, the Righteous Judge, will give to me on that day, and not to me only but also to all who have loved His appearing."* Quickened, Rasta wondered, "Is there any hope for me?" ... He was snatched away. This time Rasta wept openly as he was dragged back into his foul collection of skin and bones. The compassion pouring out of Anzel's eyes attached itself to Rasta as the demonic spirits used their waning grip on him...to try to wrench away any hope of a changing heart.

It took some professional footwork for Ella to get the hospital to release Dijin. She signed every paper they threw at her to disconnect them from any possibility of a lawsuit. Three hours later, she wheeled a proud looking hospital escapee to the front entrance. Unfortunately, Dijin's clothing didn't make the trip, having to be cut off of his swollen and feverish body. Ella, not having a clue that they would be leaving the hospital so early and under these circumstances, did not have time to fix this. Bellview was gracious enough to lend him a pair of faded scrubs and a snug looking hospital gown. Thankfully Dijin's track shoes survived the ordeal. Pulling away from the curb, Ella felt Dijin tugging at her sleeve. Turning, she looked at him questioningly. "Ella, honey, I know you're having a tough time trying to believe all of this, but I need you to reflect on the part of the marriage vows, that is very unpopular these days. The part that asks, "Are you willing to obey?" Watching Ella's light gray eyes snap and crackle to a darker gray, he hurried on, "I feel that same urgency to check on Katrina Martinez, I have to make sure that she's alright. We owe that much to everyone in our flock, and to Anzel." "But Dijin, you can't go running around like that. What about your clothes?" Ella asked nervously. "Clothes, smothes," he kidded an un amused Ella. "Okay Dijin, but don't you dare say I didn't warn you!" Merging into the thick traffic, Ella peeked over at her husband, who had his eyes closed as his lips moved in silent prayer. Suddenly, the powerful urge to pray in the spirit, fell on her as she maneuvered her way through the speeding cars…The words, restoration, healing, and wholeness, became a litany as she picked up speed and raced towards the Martinez's home.

Joints locked by indecision, Pila stared at Katrina's terrified, bloody form. She didn't know whether to approach the now whimpering woman or call the nine eleven emergency number. There was so much dried blood. But who's blood. That was the confusing part. She dialed, from where she was frozen by the door. Besides, a very angry looking lump on the side of Katrina's head, she couldn't see any visible wounds on Mrs. Martinez, but she could have some internal damage. The operator distracted her momentarily. When she opened her mouth to explain why she might need an ambulance, Katrina spoke in a calm but firm tone. "Please hang up the phone, I don't need to go to the hospital, I'm fine….now." Pila did a double take at the slowly rising Katrina. "Mrs. Martinez, maybe you should lie down until the ambulance arrives." "No need for that, now please cancel it." Not used to taking orders from her patients or their families, Pila shook free of her ruffled feathers and shrugged, disconnecting the operator, realizing that she was on hold anyway. Clearing her throat, she asked cautiously, "How can I be of help Katrina? Your parents are waiting for news of your well being." Gesturing to her cell phone she said, "May I?" The sharp, negative jerk of Katrina's head surprised her. Katrina stared down at the dried blood on her arms and legs and deeply shuddered. Her voice was barely a whisper, and with a bleak look in her eyes, she asked Pila this, "Doctor Thomas, do you believe that there is a place called hell?" "Excuse me?" Pila responded, not knowing what else to say. "I asked you if you believe in a place called hell. Do you think that such a place exists? I mean, of course you have to believe in God, and you would have to believe that He sent His only Son to die for us, so that we wouldn't have to go to such a terrible place like that…oh, but you don't believe, do you? No, I can see it on your face, you think I'm hysterical." Katrina was talking fast and rubbing her arms up and down, and right across the room from where Pila still stood, she could see the gooseflesh on Katrina. "Katrina, what kind of medication did you ingest, and how many did you take?" Pila asked, trying to maintain her professional authority. Katrina's eyes quickly dropped to the bedroom floor. "None, nada, not one pill."

Carefully approaching her Pila asked, "Katrina, may I help you to a chair and get you some water?" Looking at her suspiciously, Katrina nodded and held out a trembling hand. Water, that's what started this whole thing. She thought nervously. As Pila helped her, she took note of her frailty. "Do you remember the last time you have had anything to eat Katrina?" Looking confused for a moment, she shook her head no. "Well let's go into the kitchen to see what I can whip up for you." Katrina looked as if she was going to protest but Pila was ready to do battle over this one. Sighing in resignation she held tightly to Pila's hand. When they were almost to the kitchen door, Katrina doubled over and her knees buckled. Pila fought to keep her on her feet, but Katrina began to moan and thrash around. Seizure? Pila wracked her brain for seizure procedures. As she grappled with the frenzied Katrina, and tried to reach for her cell phone, the doorbell began to ring…Pila did the next best thing to calling for help…she called for help.

Dijin and Ella heard the yell coming from inside the Martinez's house, and without hesitating, Dijin tried the front door and paused long enough to command Ella to go back to their car and call for help if he did not come back out in sixty seconds. Ella clamped the reply on her lips and shook her head yes. Surprised at the unlocked door, Dijin said a quick prayer and barreled into the house. He immediately took in the scene near the kitchen entrance. Backtracking to the front door, he motioned Ella inside. Rushing back to assist the stranger with the struggling Katrina, he reached out and grabbed Katrina's flailing arms and said, "In the name of Jesus, I command peace in this vessel of the Lord Jesus Christ. I apply the blood of Jesus to Katrina Martinez and I declare that she is completely healed

and delivered by His stripes. Her body, soul and spirit are renewed by the power of The Most High God." Pila sat back on
her heels appalled by this fanatic, display. What did this fruit-
cake think he was doing? Katrina needed an ambulance. She
needed to be rushed to the emergency room...she...she...
was...not thrashing around anymore. She was completely
calm and staring at the strange man. She was wearing such
a look of peace on her face and...and...she was smiling? The
man and the woman both had their eyes closed and their lips
were moving. They, not realizing that Katrina was alright gave
Pila a chance to study them. The man was wearing a pair of
hospital scrubs under a hospital gown and tennis shoes. There
was a hospital band on his wrist. Curious, was he an escapee?
The woman's clothing was normal, though slightly soiled and
wrinkled. What had just happened here? There was something
going on, something very strange. A sudden change in the atmosphere made Pila's heart race as panic tried to rise in her
throat. She fought a desperate urge to flee for her...life? What
was she afraid of? It was only a man and woman, clearly in
their fifties, albeit odd. The strange man took that instant to
open his eyes and look directly into Pila's eyes. The compassion and love shining out of his eyes peeled back the layers that
Pila had spent years building around her heart. Time seemed
to freeze as Pila was transported back to her childhood. Her
hand nervously fluttered near her heart as she remembered at
age four, her maternal grandmother, rocking her on her lap
and telling her about a *kitaab* (book) in which a divine man,
a great, *Adhyaapak* (Teacher), died a terrible death to free his
people. What had it all meant? Why was she remembering her
Daa-dee-maa now? She hadn't thought of her in so many years.

She'd all but forgotten her. She vaguely remembered that there was some anger between her parents and Daa-dee-maa, and that she never saw her again after the age of five. The stranger's voice broke the spell. "C'mon, let's get Katrina up and help her over to the couch shall we?" Pila shook the cobwebs out of her head and reached out to help with Katrina. "Dijin, Ella!" Katrina cried with such pure joy and relief, that Pila dropped her in surprise. "Pastor Dijin, you came for me, but how did you know?" Pila assumed she meant presently. Grabbing Dijin and clinging to him, Kartina laughed and cried and laughed some more. "How did you know I was there Pastor? Why would you come to such a horrible place? Did God send you? Pila and Ella were looking back and forth between Dijin and Katrina...Dijin looked at all of their faces wearily, "Let's all sit down this is going to take the Lord's help to sort out.

In the spiritual realm, the demonic horde whimpered and cringed, knowing the punishment they would receive for their failure to utterly possess the subject, Katrina Martinez. As they were whipped asunder into agonized, ragged, bloody pieces, they knew as their putrid, severed limbs, burst into flames, that this was only a small sample of their anguish to come. Therefore, many of the detached heads, grinned insanely as they fell into the gross, fiery darkness. The Angelic host was allowed to continue with their cheers and rejoicing amongst their ranks. Sensing the silent command to regroup, the holy host resumed their position as they watched the filthy enemy replace their unfortunate comrades...This particular battle was not over.

Chapter 21

'The Nitty Gritty'

Rasta's returning bellow caused Anzel to rear back in surprise. "No, no, nooooo!" On his hands and knees now, he looked up at Anzel in rage and hatred. "Why are you torturing me like this? Let me die. Please if you have any feelings...just let me go." Feeling the Spirit urging him to continue the story of the Apostle Paul, he looked at the pitiful residue of the man before him with the greatest compassion he'd ever felt in his life. It had to be supernatural. Words began to whisper around Anzel as his mouth kept moving with the words of Paul's life. "Keep watching, the time is near. The love agape' will be made manifest in my son, Rasta. He is my son, my child, the very one that I have given my life for. Look at him. My church would not have chosen this man. Would they have looked on him with my eyes of mercy? Would they have found something of value in him? Would they have left their beautiful temples and fine houses in search of him? Would they recognize My presence in the dwelling places of those like this man?" The righteous indignation of The Lord's words, whipped at Anzel's soul and he wound his arms around his head as the disappointment of The Creator, for His creation, almost rent his senses in two. Just as quickly, it was gone, and a blanket of mercy and grace fell heavily across Anzel's shoulders, and he wept with gratitude. Anzel tried to communicate the love of The Father to Rasta, who had backed away and was shivering violently. The

Lord was speaking to Anzel again. "I have one final destination for Rasta Jones. This is the one which will be the key to where he will choose to spend eternity. Pray for your brother, pray for the soul that was twinned together with your soul from your mother's wombs. It is The Thinning, It is the love agape', and it will...cost you...everything!" Erupting from the belly of Anzel Martinez, from his spirit and complete essence, every word, deed and thought crystallized into a yes. A yes so pure, so selfless and passionate, that he was granted a look into the spiritual realm, and he witnessed a standing ovation from the King of Kings and the host of heaven...Anzel fainted dead away on his feet.

The atmosphere in the Martinez's living room was charged with an invisible electricity that was causing Pila to tap her feet together nervously. Dijin cleared his throat and began to make introductions. "My name is Dijin Lockhart, and this pretty, young thing is my wife, Ella." Pila couldn't help smiling as Ella blushed, ever so sweetly. "I am Doctor Pila Thomas," she said extending a trembling hand. "I have been counseling the Martinez's for a short time." Speaking up, Dijin countered with, "I have been pasturing them for a number of years." Ella cleared her throat, and gave Dijon a warning look. Looking sheepish, he glanced at Pila with an apologetic expression and took her offered hand and said, "It's so very nice to make your acquaintance." Then, continuing to hold Pila's hand, he peered into her face. Squirming in embarrassment, she looked helplessly at Ella and Katrina. Ella gave her a sympathetic look and a slight shrug. Softly, Dijin said, "I have never met you before, but I think that you are the woman that The Lord, had me praying for so urgently." Twisting her hand away, Pila's voice

prickled as she snapped, "Look Pastor Lockhart, I don't believe in all of this prayer mumbo jumbo. Someone tried to
brainwash me with that kind of talk when I was a young girl,
but..." Dijin's sudden glassy, faraway look, stopped her words.
His next statement literally knocked the breath out of her.
"I hear The Lord speaking to my heart. A long time ago God
used your grandmother to plant a tiny seed in your heart. He
then sent a Miss Lou to till the soil of His word in your heart.
Although the shepherd and the flock were weak, He used Miss
Lou to win many souls for His kingdom." Pila was experiencing
one of her rare moments of speechlessness. Dijin continued in
that strange monotone. "He wants you to know that He has
always had a plan and a purpose for your life. He was there
when you lost your sister." He paused at her sharp intake of
breath. "Yes, your sister Ryia, her death as well as your parents deaths, grieved His heart too." Pila buried her face in her
hands and broke down, sobbing. Great wrenching sobs, that
threatened her hold on her own sanity. A dam had burst inside
of Doctor Pila Thomas, a dam that she had carefully built and
guarded for so many years. Now, here she sat, in the presence
of people she barely knew, having her emotions, shamefully
exposed by a near, stranger. Soon after her parents died, her
fountain had dried up. She hadn't cried when her physician
had declared her barren, or when her husband had left her
for his young secretary. She hadn't even cried in any of her
therapy sessions. She'd only cried, when the cruelty of Rasta
mocking her sister's death had begun to manifest itself in her
life, lately. Even then her tears had brought her great shame,
and she'd hid. Dijin's voice broke through her thoughts. "The
dreams, daughter, the dreams are all a part of His plan. It is

not accidental that your path has crossed with Anzel and Rasta, the boys and Anzel and Rasta, the men. This will not be something that you will find in your textbooks, or something you can analyze. You worship gods made of things that come from what God The Father has created. You look for answers from objects that do not have life. Someone once shared the truth with you. It was your Daa-dee-maa. She shared the seed of The Eternal Father with you. Out of your lineage, you were chosen to be a servant of The Lord. Doctor Pila Thomas, The Lord is speaking to you through me right now. Harden not your heart, but choose this day, whom you will serve." Looking up at Dijin with pleading eyes, Pila asked, "How can I choose God? Please explain it to me. I just know that I'm tired of trying to live on my own, doing things my own way...so tired." Ella and Katrina circled Pila and started praying softly. Pulling a trembling Pila to her feet, Dijin looked into her eyes as the fire of holiness shone on his face. "Ask child, and you shall receive, seek and you shall find, knock and the door shall be opened to you." Understanding began to dawn in Pila's mind as Dijin continued, "If you confess with your mouth, The Lord Jesus, and believe in your heart that God raised Him from the dead, you shall be saved!" Looking at the joy and anticipation shining out of each face surrounding her, broke something open in Pila's heart. There was an odd feeling of having her sight and hearing restored. Pila looked at her hands and feet in childlike amazement. Her head was bobbing up and down, signaling, yes! "Yes, yes I do believe in my heart that Jesus was raised from the dead." Suddenly, the impact of what she was doing hit Pila and an overwhelming remorse for all of the wrong choices that she'd made in her life, smote her heart. "Ah God, please forgive me!" She wept unashamedly, falling to her knees. The hatred, jealousy and indifference for her fellow man abraded her tender newness. She bawled even louder when the truth about her marriage was pushed to the forefront of her mind. She had chosen her career over her own marriage, and the truth was that she was too selfish and self centered to desire any children. Dijin, Ella and Katrina moved away from Pila to allow The Lord to finish His work on her. A weak and slightly disoriented Katrina excused herself to go clean up and put on fresh clothing. She returned with one of Anzel's running suits for Dijin to change into. Dijin looked from the suit to his considerably larger frame and shrugged and went to change. Ella volunteered to make a fresh pot of coffee. Twenty minutes later, Pila shined a puffy and tearstained face at the small group, busily sipping cups of coffee across the room. The new joy and peace of The Lord shined out of her red rimmed eyes. Pila was pleased to see Katrina in fresh attire, and amused to see Dijin's get up. "I have a confession to make." She began shyly as fresh tears sprung from her eyes. "I don't fully understand yet, what has happened to me today." She stopped and swallowed hard, to regain some composure. "I do acknowledge today, that there is a God, Who sent His Son to die for my sins. I do want to know more about Him. Phew! Just give me a few minutes and a lifetime to get used to this." Pila visibly relaxed as everyone laughed with her. Then they were surrounding her and showering her with a degree of affection that she was totally unaccustomed to. They were hugging and kissing her. "Welcome to the family of God, dear sister, welcome home.

She truly felt like she had come home at last. Nothing would ever make her leave home again...There were two thunderous sounds in the spiritual realm, Great rejoicing and applause, and hideous screaming and the gnashing of teeth.

Chapter 22

'Were Going In'

In the ICU at Bellview Community Hospital, the comatose body of Rasta Jones jerked and bucked in the throes of a violent seizure. The medical team, looked at each other helplessly, then they went back to work on what they each secretly felt... was a lost cause and a waste of the state's funding.

When he fully revived, Anzel saw Rasta's unmoving form and allowed the Holy Spirit to pray through him with groanings which could not be uttered. An agony gripped his heart and pierced him to his soul. Through his grief for Rasta, Anzel heard these words, "Twins of the spirit, darkness and light, good and evil, two die for the good of the one, twins of the soul, A Thinning. Die? Two die? Me die? A fresh grief washed over Anzel for the loss of his family. Just as quickly, the Spirit separated it from him. "Everything!"...The word shook Anzel and he regained his focus, and continued praying for Rasta.

Rasta was set again into Paul the Aged. His sigh of relief was cut short when he noticed his surroundings. Fear sent his heart into a wild gallop, when he realized that his hands were tightly bound behind his back. His arms felt nearly wrenched from their sockets as he was shoved to his knees. Frantically searching Paul's thoughts, he found a peace that confounded his own terror. Startling information shook him to the core. Emperor Nero had ordered the execution of Paul and many more Christians. The Apostle had narrowly escaped the cruel torture of crucifixion, because of his Roman citizenship. They were now at 'Agave Selviae'. Rasta was horrified. Even in this painful position, possibly minutes away from an axe coming down on his neck, Paul's thoughts amazed him. Paul was praying. He was asking God to forgive him for anything that he had done, anything that had offended Him. He prayed for the souls of his brothers and sisters, who were facing the hour of their departure along with him. Departure? Departure? They weren't going on a trip. Somebody was going to cut their heads from their bodies. His next words captivated Rasta's heart. "Father of my heart, please forgive the ones who have brought this evil to pass. Just as my Savior spoke from his cross. "They know not what they do." They have been tricked by the adversary. Please help them to know how much you love them. Dearest Lord, I pray now also for a man who you have shown me in my deepest prayer hour. There is a man who will be born many, many years from now, in a Gentile nation, far away. He will be ensnared as a child, by the enemy of our souls. He will wander, for a time, in gross darkness, not knowing that you have attached him to a brother of the light. I pray that he will take the hand of deliverance that you will hold out to him. These things I pray, in the name of The Father, The Son and The Holy Ghost. Now Lord, I commit my soul into Your hands. I have run my course, I have finished my..." Rasta felt the sharp edge of the executioner's axe slice into the back of his neck as he was snatched back into his own body. The scream on Rasta's lips, turned into cries of relief for his own escape and regret for the fate of the Apostle Paul. "Why would he pray for everyone like that? Even his enemies, even...me?" The demonic hold on Rasta was very weak now. There was a clearing going on in his mind, a new reasoning that was fortified by the absence of black hatred. Then regret began to grow in Rasta's heart. Sorrow for the pain and destruction, he had poured on everyone in his path. "Oh God!" Rasta screamed. This was unbearable. The faces of his countless victims, danced in front of his eyes. All of the hateful, hurtful, evil things that he had inflicted, played out in detail. "Stop!" He tried to cry, but no sound came out. Curling in upon himself, he wept like a baby because he was finally, able to be sorry...truly, helplessly, heart rending, inescapably, sorry! Sorry! Sorry!

Ninety minutes later, Katrina's dining room table was hidden beneath pizza boxes, napkins and greasy, empty paper plates. Katrina's plate was the only one that remained untouched, as she recounted her terrifying visit to hell. Pila's eyes were as round as saucers as she listened to Katrina conclude with the astounding rescue by Dijin Lockhart. Dijin listened to Katrina without interruption. His only response was several head nods and rapid eye blinks. "Oh Dijin, I didn't believe you, I thought you were hallucinating. Can you ever forgive me?" Ella asked, as she stood and went quickly over to her husband and lifted his weary face. Studying his clouded eyes, she placed her hand on his brow and began to pray for him. "Oh great and mighty God, Creator of all things, bless this faithful warrior with strength in his spirit. Thank you for using him in this unique way and rescuing our dear spiritual daughter. Father, You have not revealed to us Your plan concerning Anzel, but we trust You with our loved ones. Thank you for our new sister in Christ, sister Pila. Lord, what do we do now? What is Your will for us, your four children that you have brought together in this place? Speak to us Jesus." Silence fell thickly around the dining room. The only sound was the ticking of the grandfather clock in the foyer. Ella returned softly to her seat, sensing the presence of The Holy Ghost. No one moved. Pila's eyes darted from face to face with her brows knit in puzzlement. Katrina stared at her hands in her lap. Ella's eyes were closed, as she barely moved her lips. Dijin had his face slightly tilted to the right, as if he were listening to something or someone. Finally, breathing out a heavy sigh, Dijin said, "Yes Lord, let Your will be done." Pila, Ella and Katrina, startled him as they asked in unison, "What'd He say?" Biting back a nervous chuckle, Dijin put up both hands as if to protect himself. "Hold on ladies, give me a chance to sort some things out. All kidding aside, we need to cover ourselves with spiritual protection and get back to Bellview Hospital." He held up a hand to stop Ella's protests, I know I've just been released from the same hospital but you're just going to have to bite the bullet, because the Lord wants us to sneak back into the hospital and into the Intensive Care Unit, to pray for Rasta Jones." "Surely He didn't use the word sneak." Ella said. "Well whatever word He used, that unction was placed in my spirit. C'mon ladies, chop, chop! Rasta's not long for this world. We must get to him in time and help make sure that he is ready to stand before The Lord." The seriousness of his words moved everyone into action, gathering coats and bags, they headed for the door. Katrina insisted on calling her parents to let them know she was alright. As they were pulling into traffic in Doctor Thomas's little green car, Pila turned to Dijin and warned him in a low tone, "You are probably not aware Pastor Lockhart, but there is always an armed guard posted outside of Rasta's room. After all he is a dangerous criminal. Also only family or medical personnel are allowed in the room." To Pila's consternation, Dijin simply smiled as though he had some sort of mysterious secret. Feeling her frustration, he offered her this, "Doctor Thomas, there are so many things that you are not ready to absorb concerning the workings of salvation. You are still like a newborn baby, with a long journey ahead of you. I on the other hand, have been walking with God for many years now, and I still haven't scratched the surface of the marvelous things He has in store for us. Let me give you this sound advice. Study His word, connect with fellow believers who love The Lord, seek His will for yourself, develop a strong and healthy prayer life and learn to have faith in Him, because without faith it is impossible to please Him. If He sent us on this heavenly mission, He will open up the way to get His work done." Falling silent, Dijin did not speak again until they had found an discreet parking space at the hospital…"What have I gotten myself into now?" Pila asked herself silently.

⚓

Pity for the broken creature before him almost undid Anzel. A powerful quickening in his spirit jarred him and shook his entire body, as heat and light spread throughout him, blinding Rasta. A supernatural love for his brother expanded his heart to it's human limit, *his brother!* It felt so natural to him now. Looking at his hands and arms filled him with boyish mirth. How they glowed and pulsated. "Pick your brother up!" The words were commanded sharply. Rasta cowered away from Anzel's glowing hands. Speaking words, as they were given by the Holy Spirit, he said, "Don't be afraid, brother, God loves you!" "Why should God love me? I'm just a filthy piece of garbage. It's too late for me isn't it?" Rasta asked, sounding very much like a small child. Being filled with all of the authority, allowed to a messenger of God, Anzel lifted himself up to his fullest height and said, "Make your choice brother. Will it be heaven or hell, darkness or light, God or Satan, agony or joy unspeakable peace…or unrest?"…With both hands extended towards Rasta, Anzel waited, watched and prayed.

After holding hands and praying in the hospital parking lot, Pila was filled with a certainty that Doctor Maylon Tessker would understand their request and make it possible to visit Rasta Jones' room. Pulling out her cell phone, she dialed his number and heaved a sigh of relief when he answered on the third ring. Before Pila could utter her bizarre request, Doctor Tessker amazed her by saying, "Doctor Thomas, you probably won't believe me, but as I was sitting here in my office, an overwhelming burden of prayer came over me. The burden was for you, and three others whom I'm not familiar with, along with patient Jones. The Lord has instructed me to assist you in any way possible. Confirmation came just now, when the phone rang." As Pila described to him what their assignment was, and shared her newly found conversion…Doctor Tessker rocked back in his chair and expelled a loud "WHEW!"

True to his word, Doctor Tessker met the disheveled group as they stepped off of the elevator to the ICU wing. Looking at Pila, he said offhandedly, "When this is over will you allow me to buy you a cup of coffee, so that we can talk about the outcome of things? After all, I had to pull a lot of strings to make this happen." Pila self consciously smoothed back her unkempt bob, while she studied the attractive, older doctor. Expertly assessing his left hand for signs of a wedding ring, without his knowledge, she gave him a giant grin. "You have my promise and I will pay for the coffee, and even throw in a pastry." He held out his hand for a shake, to seal the deal, and blushed slightly as an amused Dijin, cleared his throat. Waving goodbye to the group, he headed quickly for the elevators. "I'll be praying for you, page me if you run into any difficulties." He said through closing elevator doors. Finding the nurse's station empty the group sought Rasta's room, which was easily identified by the guard standing in front of the door. Nervously they approached the unsmiling officer who kept one hand near his weapon. When they reached the officer, he stepped aside without a word and opened the door and gestured them inside. The four arrivals let out a collective gasp at the apparition on the bed. Cautiously they approached Rasta's bedside, making various sounds of sympathy and pity. Over the sounds of the life saving machines, Rasta gasped for each precious breath. He was awake. Wheezing like some animal in the final throes of death. Looking pensive, Dijin spoke softly, "There's not much time." Rasta looked at Dijin knowingly. Leaning close to Rasta's face, Dijin asked, "Mr. Jones, do you know the whereabouts of Anzel Martinez?" Something moved in Rasta's expression, panic? Then his expression became blank. Dijin hesitated, as he felt The Lord leading him to plead with Rasta, to embrace His Son, Jesus in his last few minutes of life. "Rasta, I am a pastor, and The Lord sent us here today to share the gospel of salvation with you. Would you like to know The Lord Jesus, in the pardon of your sins?" Rasta's eyes widened, and his expression became, heartbreakingly tragic. His lips began to tremble as huge tears welled up in his eyes. He made guttural sounds as he tried to speak. The more he tried to form words, the more he labored to breathe. Resembling a trapped animal, his eyes darted wildly from one face to another. Fixing his stare on Katrina, his body began to stop fighting against the inevitable, and he began to relax. Fascinated, Katrina moved closer to Rasta's line of vision. Slowly moving his lips, Rasta began to speak in a dry, raspy voice. What he said caused Katrina to desperately clutch the hospital bed railing, to keep from falling. His eyes surprisingly clear now he stared hard at Katrina and said, *"I go by the name of Ricky Plain!"* In that instant, Katrina knew, in her heart, that God had answered her prayers and sent her assurance that Anzel was alright. Somehow through these wasted scraps of flesh and bone, God was sending a message. The Holy Ghost whispered urgently into her spirit to speak to Rasta, the words He would give her, and to do it quickly. Katrina swallowed her natural revulsion to the sight and smell of Rasta's decaying body. She deliberately cleared her mind of the knowledge of his ruthless life and many victims. Feeling a check in her spirit, she paused as the little ICU, began to vibrate as all sound was sucked out, and they were seemingly in a vacuum. They stared wide eyed at each other not daring to break the heavy silence. Allowing the Spirit of The Lord to take the lead, Katrina reached trembling hands over the railing and cupped Rasta's ravaged, barely human face. Rasta stared, unblinkingly into her eyes as his light began to dim. Humbling herself for this assignment, Katrina became the embodiment of everyone of Rasta's victims. Softly she spoke the final words, to free Rasta from the prison of his wretched body and tragic life.... *"I forgive you."* Rasta stiffened, and a loud guttural, "NO!" broke the thick silence of the ICU. The room began to fill with the smell of burning sulfur, as

Rasta bucked and twisted with such force that the hospital bed threatened to collapse. Strangely calm, Katrina gestured for Dijin, Ella and Pila to grab hands and as a bizarre wind began to whip around the tight little group, she led them in a song that she used to sing in Sunday school, as a child. "Jesus' blood washed the whole world clean. He searched through the darkness and reached in for me. My sins made me filthy, nothing else could erase. But my beautiful Savior, held out His sweet grace. Oh, the blood, the blood from the cross on the hill. The blood, the blood, it cleanses me still." The fearless foursome held on to each other and sang the litany over and over again. Incredibly, the guard at the door appeared to have been asleep on his feet since Rasta began to speak. He had not stirred, even once. Soon, heavenly voices joined in until the sound of a hundred, perfect choirs filled the hospital room. Every exquisite note pierced each human heart to the core. The four warriors sobbed, brokenly through the song, but felt the push to continue. Suddenly the wind blew itself out in a violent rush that ripped and tore at the room's occupants. The door to the room violently flew open and slammed shut. They looked at each other in wide eyed shock, but no one dared to speak. Peace entered the room on heavenly wings, and hovered, lovingly around the group. A collective gasp could be heard as all eyes turned to Rasta. The filthy, yellowed, wolverine teeth began to recede as the icy blueness of his eyes, became calm and fixed on something above their heads. The familiar death rattle filled the room now, but it was peace and not panic that shown from Rasta's countenance. The corners of Rasta's lips turned up in a weak smile. Dijin would spend many nights in the years to come, wondering if the vision that he saw, as Rasta

Jones expired and went to be with his Jesus, the forgiver of sins, was real or imagined. No one else seemed to notice. Dijin was almost as positive as he was about his own name, that just for a fraction of a second, before Rasta passed, he saw the smiling face of Anzel Martinez, superimposed over Rasta's face. Before he could dwell too long on it the atmosphere was overtaken with peals of boyish laughter. Everything shimmered as the laughter grew in volume, reached an incredible crescendo, and disappeared. Feeling the Lord, release them, Dijin gathered the fearless, foursome and gently but firmly pushed them towards the door, he looked quickly at the guard and saw him stirring. He informed him of Rasta's passing and left him to make arrangements. Dijin saw the officer look at Rasta's still form with disdain and press the call button...Rasta Jones was no more in this world.

Making the right choice for the first time in his life, Rasta reached up and clasped Anzel's hands. As he was being lifted to his feet, he was infused with a feeling of having his full youthful strength back. Looking down at himself in joyful amazement, he saw that he was a young boy again, and to his delightful surprise, Anzel was also a boy again. Anzel pulled Rasta into a bear hug as they were both enveloped in the brightness of God's love and acceptance. Then they were laughing happily... as The Lord took them, and they were no more.

The group was back at Pila's car before Dijin spoke. "Dear ones, as Paul wrote in the book of Galatians chapter four and verse eighteen. *"But it is good to be zealous in a good thing always, and not only when I am present with you."*There are many more lost souls like Rasta out there, but the church is afraid or not willing to dirty its hands for the cause of Christ. Now we can

go back to our everyday lives and act as if none of these supernatural miracles has happened. I for one am changed in such
a way that I will never be the same again. Thank you Jesus."
Prayerfully, we can understand that God brought our diverse
little group together, to experience a unique soul expedition,
which took an extreme thinning of our attachment to this
world. Now we know that we can love the unlovely and show
God's mercy to the merciless and see some value in the despi-
cable." Holding out his hands, and using his pulpit voice, Dijin
thundered, "Who's with me?" Trembling slightly, Pila was the
first one to grasp Dijin's upraised hand. Looking a trifle miffed
at her husband's theatrics, Ella stepped up next. Lastly, shivering uncontrollably, Katrina, studied each of her dear friends
and with her restored joy shining out of her eyes she stepped
forward and clasped hands with them. She knew that Anzel
would be very proud of his little hot tamale…and she would
do whatever it took to see him in glory.

THE END

(Author's note)

Dear reader, This book was a great love story between the Creator of the universe and the lost. Each one of us who have embraced the sacrifice of Jesus Christ, was in some sense a type of Rasta Jones. I can remember the Anzels and Dijins in my own life. I was very resistant to rescue at times, but I thank God for His persistence and mercy. That great lover of my soul chased me and wooed me and He has captured my heart for all eternity! My prayer for you, reader is that you will seek the leading of the Holy Spirit, today. Someone needs your help. I strongly believe God has assigned souls to each one of us in His service. He is calling for His hands and feet in the earth to lift His fallen children up out of darkness and help lead them into His marvelous light. There is an urgency! Listen for your instructions today and may God bless you for your obedience, in Jesus name I pray. Amen.

(Thinning Discussion Questions)

1. Do you personally believe in spiritual warfare?

2. Have you ever had a personal encounter with an angel or demon?

3. Have you ever met someone similar to the character Rasta?

4. Do you pray earnestly for the lost? Has this story influenced you to begin?

5. What is the greatest sacrifice you have ever made for someone else?

6. What has God called you to do?

7. Do you believe that there is a heaven and a hell?

8. Would you recognize the voice of The Lord?

9. Can God count on your obedience for whatever He asks of you?

10. Do you believe God is in control of your destiny?

11. Has the Holy Spirit ever given you the unction to approach someone you would usually avoid?

12. Are you familiar with the bible's teachings on love?

13. Do you believe that you can personally do more?

14. What if only God knew about your sacrifices, would you still do them?

15. 15) Do you have confidence in the Shepherd that God has placed you under?

16. Do you think that Pastor Dijin was a good shepherd for Anzel and Katrina?

17. Have you ever read of or heard of an account of someone's near death experience where they claimed to have visited hell?

18. Were you frightened by Katrina's experience?

19. Did you understand the magnitude of God's love in this story?

20. Has this story caused you to view people in a different light?